The Riddle
of
Baby Rosalind

NICKI HOLLAND MYSTERIES

The Riddle
of
Baby Rosalind

Angela Elwell Hunt

Tommy nelson™

FOR TWEENS AND TEENS

A Division of Thomas Nelson Publishers
Since 1798

www.thomasnelson.com

Published in Nashville, Tennessee, by Tommy Nelson®, a Division of Thomas Nelson, Inc. Visit us on the Web at www.tommynelson.com.

Scripture quotations are from the *International Children's Bible*®, *New Century Version*®, copyright © 1986, 1988, 1999 by Tommy Nelson®, a Division of Thomas Nelson, Inc.

Tommy Nelson® books may be purchased in bulk for educational, business, fund-raising, or sales promotional use. For information, please e-mail SpecialMarkets@ThomasNelson.com.

This is a work of fiction. Names, characters, places, and incidents either are the product of the author's imagination or are used fictitiously.

Interior: Jennifer Ross / MJ Ross Design

ISBN 1-4003-0771-6

Printed in the United States of America
05 06 07 08 09 WRZ 9 8 7 6 5 4 3 2 1

One

1:00 PM Ireland Time
8:00 AM Eastern Standard Time

"We're going to miss the plane, girls, if we don't hurry," Mrs. Cushman told Nicki Holland and her friends as they lifted their suitcases from the trunk of a taxi. "Does everybody have everything?"

Laura Cushman counted her bags out loud: "One suitcase, one makeup case, one hanging bag, and three souvenir cases." She nodded. "I've got everything, Mama."

Christine Kelshaw elbowed Kim Park. "How about you?" she asked. "Do you have all thirty-six of your suitcases?"

Kim smiled. "No," she said, ducking her head in embarrassment. "I only have two."

"That was Christine's attempt to make a joke, Kim," Meredith Dixon explained, heaving her suitcase onto the baggage cart Nicki had wheeled over. "American humor often relies on exaggeration."

"When you explain everything, Meredith, you take the fun out of the joke," Christine complained, patting the strip of gray duct tape that kept the seams of her battered suitcase together. "And what's your scientific opinion of my patch job? Will my suitcase make it back home to the good old US of A?"

1

"If your suitcase made it from England to Ireland, it ought to arrive safe and sound in Tampa," Meredith answered, amusement lurking in her dark eyes. "Your suitcase looked like that when we began this trip, didn't it?"

"Yeah." Christine patted the large plaid suitcase with affection. "Mom said I could either have spending money or buy a new suitcase, so you can guess which one I chose. There was absolutely no way I was going on this trip without cash!"

"You know, we ought to think of something nice to do for Mrs. Cushman once we get home," Nicki whispered as she put her bag next to the others'. "If she hadn't come up with this trip to Europe as part of Laura's birthday present, none of us would even be here."

"And we wouldn't have had the opportunity to solve a couple of great mysteries," Meredith added.

Kim blushed. "Especially the secret of Cravenhill Castle."

Nicki noticed the blush and smiled. "I know you're thinking of Trant Shea back on Cravenhill Island," she said, teasing. "He promised to write, didn't he? Who knows, maybe you'll have the chance to see him sooner than you think."

Mrs. Cushman clapped to get the girls' attention. "Is everything loaded?" She peered inside the taxi for any bags that might have been left behind. "Well, then, we're off to the currency exchange, then to the gift shops, then onto the plane. With luck and a good tail wind, we'll be home by nine o'clock tonight."

"I never thought I'd look so forward to seeing Pine Grove

again," Nicki said, grabbing the handle of the luggage cart. "But I actually miss the place."

"Me, too," Meredith admitted. "It feels like I haven't seen my mom and dad in months, and it's only been a week."

"A week without my five brothers and sisters is pure heaven," Christine said as they walked into the busy Dublin airport. "But I have to admit it will be nice to sleep in my own bed for a change. I don't know why, but I'm really tired."

Nicki thought of her five-year-old brother, Joshua, and six-year-old sister, Sarah, who waited at home. Had they missed her? Sometimes she felt more like their built-in baby-sitter than their sister, but she had missed them. And while it had been nice to have Mrs. Cushman and other adults around on this trip, it would be great to see her own mom and dad again.

"Nicki, hurry up," Laura called over her shoulder. Nicki quickened her pace and gave the cart a mighty shove. In about twelve hours, after a long flight across the Atlantic Ocean, she'd be back home.

―

The girls checked their luggage, showed the attendant their passports and plane tickets, then moved toward the currency exchange booths. While Mrs. Cushman had a wad of Irish pounds to convert back into American dollars, Nicki rummaged around in her purse and could only come up with two one-pound coins and several smaller pieces of change.

The girl behind the desk smiled ruefully. "I'm sorry, but we don't convert coins," she said. "Why don't you have a look around in the gift shop before you go? Take home an Irish souvenir for your family."

"Thanks, I'll do that," Nicki said, moving away.

In the gift shop, Christine eyed a box of chocolates. "What do you think?" She pointed to a small box. "Would that last me all the way home?"

"The way you eat, it will last five minutes," Nicki answered. "After all we've eaten on this trip, I'm going to skip desserts for a month or I'll never fit into my clothes."

"Just hold your gut in." Christine took the box of candy from the shelf. "That's what I do."

Meredith walked up in time to hear Christine's last comment. She was holding a book, *222 Fabulous Factoids*. "Look what I found," she said, waving the book in front of Nicki and Christine. "This is great stuff. In late-nineteenth-century France there lived a man who had exceptional control over all his muscles. He could make his belly stick out or draw it in to the point that he looked like a human skeleton."

Christine grinned. "I can almost do that. What's the big deal?"

"This guy could even shut off the blood from the right side of his body and control the beating of his heart," Meredith said, turning a page. "I don't think you can quite do that."

"Meredith's lecturing again, isn't she?" Laura asked, coming over with her mother and Kim. "She's got that schoolteacher look on her face."

"It's interesting stuff, I guess," Nicki said, picking up two small trolls from the gift shop shelf. "What do you think about these? Will Joshua and Sarah like these Irish trolls?"

"Everybody likes trolls," Kim said, the dimple in her cheek deepening. "Trant gave me one with purple hair before we left this morning."

Laura lifted an eyebrow in Kim's direction. "And you didn't tell us! What else happened when you told your new boyfriend good-bye?"

"Nothing." Kim blushed again. "He gave me the troll, we promised to write, and we said good-bye."

"Speaking of trolls, did you know about Richeborg, the twenty-three-inch dwarf who spied as a secret agent during the French Revolution?" Meredith asked, reading from her book. "They dressed him up like a baby." She grinned. "This is great. I'm going to buy this book so I'll have something to read on the plane."

"Tell us about it later, dear," Mrs. Cushman said, checking her watch. "If you want to buy gifts, girls, hurry along. We need to make our way down to the gate if we don't want to miss our flight."

By the time they settled into chairs in the gate area, Christine had eaten her chocolate and was complaining of a sore throat and a runny nose. Mrs. Cushman produced two aspirin from her purse. "There's a water fountain over there, Chris." She pointed down the long corridor. "Take these, then you can rest on the plane. I hate to take you home sick—what will your parents think?"

"Are these all your children?" a small woman in a nearby seat asked, and Mrs. Cushman shook her head in a definite no. "My daughter and her friends," she explained, pointing to Laura, Nicki, Kim, Meredith, and Christine. "We took a trip to London together. We're from Pine Grove, Florida."

"I am visiting the United States," the woman answered in a lilting Irish accent. Nicki didn't intend to eavesdrop, but she couldn't help overhearing the women's conversation. "My name is Megan O'Connor," she said, fidgeting with her purse strap. "My husband won a visa to emigrate to the United States last year and now I am finally able to join him."

"You'll like the United States," Mrs. Cushman answered smoothly. "There's nothing to worry about. You'll adjust well, I'm sure."

As they continued to make pleasant conversation, Nicki studied Mrs. O'Connor. She was tiny, probably only five feet tall, and her shoulder-length red hair was neatly pulled back by a headband. She was dressed in a white cotton blouse and skirt and her fair skin had obviously never seen a Florida beach.

"Have you ever seen such pale skin?" Nicki whispered to Meredith.

Meredith made a face. "Who cares what color her skin is?"

Nicki looked at Meredith's dark skin and smiled. "You're

right. I guess I'm just used to everyone in Florida. Even the people who stay out of the sun have skin darker than hers."

Nicki forgot about Mrs. O'Connor as another woman approached the gate. This woman carried herself with the grace and attitude of a queen on animperial visit. As the woman handed her ticket to the flight attendant at the check-in counter, Nicki was vaguelyreminded of the lady who anchored the evening news ontelevision. As she tapped her nails on the counter and waited for her boarding pass, the blonde woman nodded gracefully to the attendant and absently adjusted the narrow lapels on her pencil-slim red suit. She was impeccably dressed, with a thin leather briefcase as her only accessory.

"What do you think about her?" Meredith asked, nodding gently toward the blonde. "I say she's a professional—maybe a lawyer."

"A red suit is too flashy for lawyers," Nicki answered. "She's in television, or maybe the movies—"

"The suit's too corporate-looking for a movie star," Meredith countered. "Maybe she's the president of a company—"

"Not the president," Laura offered, joining in the game. "If she were the president, she wouldn't be checking in at the gate, she'd be flying in a private jet. But she's definitely on the way up, not like the guy three rows back."

"What guy?" Nicki and Meredith asked.

Laura jerked her head toward a young man sitting three rows

behind the girls. He had dark, wet-looking hair pulled back into a tight ponytail, and he wore a huge brown overcoat over blue jeans and scuffed boots. His eyes darted from place to place, looking at nothing in particular, and his sharp nose looked like an exclamation point in the middle of his face.

"What about that guy?" Meredith asked.

"He's no executive," Laura whispered. "Scuffed shoes. No luggage. No briefcase. But he's too heavily dressed to be on vacation, and not dressed up enough to be on a business trip. He must be a loser."

"You can't really judge a person by the way he's dressed." Nicki folded her arms. "I'd never call someone a loser just because his shoes are scuffed."

"You'd be surprised how much you can judge a person by their appearance," Laura answered. She stood up. "I'm going to the rest room before we get on the plane. Anybody else have to go?"

Nicki, Meredith, and Kim shook their heads.

"I'll bet I'm right about that guy," Laura called as she walked away, not caring who heard her.

Nicki cringed and peeked over at the man in the overcoat. He didn't seem to be paying Laura any attention, and Nicki sighed in relief. Maybe he wasn't a loser, but Nicki had to admit Laura was probably right about one thing. The guy in the heavy overcoat didn't look like a tourist or a business-man. Something about him was wrong and strangely out of place—was it the coat? It was August, too hot for heavy clothing.

Meredith must have read Nicki's mind. "Maybe he's on his way to visit family or friends," she suggested. "You don't dress up to do that. You wear whatever's comfortable."

"Right," Nicki agreed, stretching her legs out into the aisle to get comfortable. "That makes sense."

Two

Mrs. Cushman leaned over and tapped Nicki's arm. "Nicki, honey, they're about to start boarding and Laura's not here. Could you please go into the rest room and see what's keeping her?"

"Sure." Nicki stood up and walked to the rest room nearest their gate. As soon as she turned the tiled corner, she caught a glimpse of Laura by the mirrors and sinks and the sight made her gasp. Laura was happily playing peek-a-boo in the mirror with a sweatered bundle of arms and legs.

"Is that a baby?" Nicki squealed, coming closer. She lowered her voice to an intense whisper. "Good grief, Laura, where'd you get a baby?"

Laura laughed and patted the baby's tiny hand. "Isn't she darling? Her name's Rosalind, and she really likes me. Oh, how I wish I could take her home!"

Nicki looked around. "Where's her mother?"

Laura gestured toward one of the bathroom stalls. "Don't have a cow, Nicki, her mother's in there. They came in and she asked me to hold the baby for a minute, that's all."

Nicki patted the baby's rosy cheek. "Wow, that lady must trust you a lot," she said. "I remember when my brother and sister were little—my mom watched them like a hawk."

10

The sound of running water interrupted her, then a young woman came out of the stall and headed for the sink. As she washed her hands, she smiled at Nicki and Laura. "Thank you for watching Rosalind," she said, sprigs of brown hair jutting out from beneath her knitted cap. "It's so difficult to do the simplest things when you have a baby."

"It was no trouble," Laura said, bouncing baby Rosalind in her arms. "If you're on our flight, I'd be happy to watch her for you any time."

"What flight are you on?" the young woman asked, drying her hands on a paper towel.

"The flight that leaves in twenty minutes for Atlanta," Nicki said, interrupting. "Laura, your mom sent me in here to get you. You don't want to miss the plane."

"No, I don't," Laura echoed as the woman held out her hands. Laura handed the baby to the woman and waved good-bye.

"We're on that flight, too," the woman answered. "You'll see us again, I'm sure."

Laura lingered to play peek-a-boo, and Nicki grabbed her arm and pulled her out of the rest room. "Bye—bye, baby Rosalind," Laura called as Nicki pulled her out the door. "See you soon!"

—

The flight attendant had called for the boarding of rows thirty through forty when Nicki and Laura ran up. Mrs. Cushman frowned when she saw them. "I was afraid you'd make us all late," she said, handing Laura her bag from the gift shop. "We need to get in line because they'll be calling your row next."

"Is your mom flying first class again?" Christine whispered to Laura as they took their places at the end of the long line.

"Yeah," Laura whispered. "And I'm glad. I like my mom, but sometimes it's nice when she leaves us alone, you know?"

"I know what you mean," Christine answered, wiping her red nose with a tissue. She paused a moment, then sneezed.

"Jeepers, stay away from me." Laura pulled away from Christine. "I don't want to be sick next week and miss the first day of school."

"If you're going to catch Christine's cold, you've probably already done it," Meredith said. She raised an eyebrow. "Your body is presently fighting off the germs and you'll begin to feel the results in a few hours."

Laura made a pained face, and Nicki laughed. "But if you're not going to catch a cold, you'll be just fine," Nicki added. "So don't worry about it. Let's just enjoy the flight home."

Laura elbowed Nicki. "Look, over there—there's that lady and Rosalind! See, everybody, isn't that the most darling baby? Her mother let me hold her in the rest room."

"Cute kid," Meredith agreed. "But isn't that girl awfully young to be a mother?"

Nicki looked curiously at Rosalind's mother. She had never been very good at guessing the ages of adults—someone could be twenty or thirty, she really couldn't tell. But Meredith was right.

Under the knitted cap, Rosalind's mother did seem young. Her figure was as thin and willowy as a young girl's.

Nicki gasped when she realized the woman was staring back at her. "Ohmigoodness," Nicki said, turning quickly to face Meredith. "She caught me staring at her and she's coming this way! At least I think she is. Is she? Or did she turn around?"

"She's coming this way, all right," Meredith said, looking over Nicki's shoulder. "In fact, she's here."

Nicki turned slowly. The woman stood at her elbow with the baby, and Rosalind cooed happily when she recognized Laura. "I hoped we'd see you again," the woman said, struggling to hold onto the child as the little girl reached for Laura. "And I've got to ask you for another tremendous favor. I feel a bit ill, and I've got to run into the lavatory before boarding. Will you be a dear and take the baby for me? We're seated in row fourteen, and if you could just keep the baby until I begin to feel a bit better, I'd appreciate it ever so much."

"Why, I'd love to baby-sit." Laura handed her gift shop package to Kim and reached for the baby. "Come here, precious, and let Auntie Laura entertain you for a while."

Nicki looked carefully at the pale woman. The woman's eyes were large and timid, and she did not look well. "Are you sure you're okay? Should we call a doctor or something?"

The woman squinted as if in pain and clutched at her stomach. "No, I will be fine in a moment," she said, slipping the baby's diaper bag onto Laura's free arm. "I have a nervous stomach and I always get sick before I fly. If I can just get to the lav, I'll be fine."

Before Nicki could say anything else, the woman darted off toward the restroom. Nicki looked at Meredith, and Meredith shrugged.

"A baby," Kim breathed, with a tinge of sadness in her eyes as she watched the baby. "I have never had a younger brother or sister. I know nothing about babies."

"What's to know?" Christine said, wiping her nose. "They cry, they eat, they wet their diapers and worse. The best part about baby-sitting is when their mothers come to pick them up."

Nicki laughed. "Let's just hope Rosalind's mother doesn't miss the plane."

Three

Once they were on board the huge airliner, Laura plopped down in a middle seat and let Nicki, Meredith, Kim, and Christine handle the details of settling in. With the baby in her lap, Laura played peek-a-boo and crooned pat-a-cake while Nicki and Meredith tossed their carry-on luggage, purses, and the bags from the gift shop in the plane's overhead storage bins.

When everything was put away, Nicki sat between Laura and Meredith and looked over at the baby. She had to admit the kid was cute. Rosalind had huge blue eyes that looked up and out with innocent curiosity, and her cheeks were soft and cotton-candy pink. She had a tiny rosebud mouth, and two tiny bottom teeth that gleamed when she smiled. Her little chubby fingers were constantly reaching out to touch whatever caught her interest, and a tiny tuft of blonde baby hair peeked out from under the cotton bonnet on her head.

"Isn't she adorable?" Laura playfully scolded the baby as Rosalind tried to eat a handful of Laura's long hair. "Maybe her mother will take a nap or something, and we can baby-sit the entire trip."

"I don't know if that would be much fun," Meredith said, opening her book of fabulous factoids. "It's going to take us nearly eight hours to fly home. That's a long time, especially if you've got a baby on your lap."

15

Kim dangled her necklace in front of the baby's curious gaze. "How do you know her name?"

"Her mom told me while we were in the rest room," Laura answered. "Rosalind McSomething, I don't remember her last name, but I'm sure about the Rosalind. Isn't she just like a rose? So soft and sweet, and she smells so good—"

Christine crinkled her nose. "Just wait until she fills her diaper, then let me know what you think about her smell."

Nicki took one look at Christine's red and weepy eyes and knew her friend wasn't feeling well. "After we take off, Chris, why don't you look for an empty row of seats? Then maybe you can stretch out and take a nap or something. You look like you're really sick."

"I feel like I'm really sick," Christine answered. She put her hand on her forehead. "I think I'm beginning to run a fever."

Laura threw her arm around the baby. "Then stay away from the kid, okay? You can't give your germs to her."

Christine closed her eyes. "Believe me, that's the last thing I want to do." She folded her arms across her chest and leaned back in her seat. "Don't let anyone wake me up, okay? I'm not hungry, I don't want anything to drink, and I don't want any peanuts. I just want to sit here and suffer."

Nicki tried to peer past the passengers who were still straggling into the plane, but she couldn't see much from where she sat. "Meredith, you're on the aisle, can you look up front and see anything? Has Rosalind's mother come on board yet?"

Meredith lifted herself out of her seat, then sank back down with a sigh. "I can't see anything," she said. "The seats are too high, and everyone's milling about in the front of the cabin. Some guy in sunglasses just ran in and the flight attendants are fussing over him."

"Rosalind's mom wanted to just sit and rest for a few minutes anyway, remember?" Laura said. She laughed as the baby reached for Kim's shiny necklace.

"What if she misses the plane?" Nicki asked. "What do we do then?"

"Oh come on, Nicki, do you think any woman is going to let a plane take off without her baby?" Laura asked. "No way. Besides, you met the lady—she was nice and very responsible-looking."

"Still, I'd feel better if I knew she made it on board." Nicki unfastened her seat belt. "What row did she say she was sitting in? Fourteen?"

Meredith nodded.

Nicki stood up, but was interrupted by a gentle bell that rang as the "Fasten Seat Belt" sign lit up. A flight attendant magically appeared at Nicki's elbow as if she were connected to the bell and the sign.

"I'm sorry, but you'll have to take your seat now," the flight attendant said, gesturing gracefully toward the seat belt sign. "We're beginning to taxi onto the runway."

"Can you tell me if everyone made it on board?" Nicki asked. "Are there any passengers who checked in but aren't here? I'm worried that this baby's mother—"

The flight attendant smiled and stopped Nicki with a wave of her hand. "All passengers with tickets are present and accounted for," she said firmly. "And all, except you, are in their seats."

Nicki sat down abruptly, then Laura leaned over and giggled. "I guess she told you," she whispered. "Flight attendants don't like it when you disobey the seat belt signs."

"I'm not disobeying," Nicki grumbled, fastening her seat belt again. "I was just trying to make sure we're not in major trouble with this baby."

"What kind of major trouble could we be in?" Laura asked, making wide-eyed faces at the baby. Rosalind squealed with glee and Nicki found herself smiling even though she didn't want to.

She closed her eyes. "Nothing, I guess."

—

The huge jet lifted itself into the air slowly, and as they climbed through the clouds Nicki felt her ears begin to pop. She looked around at her friends. "Does anybody have any gum? My ears are popping."

Rosalind must have felt the pressure, too, because the baby stopped smiling and began to pout. After a minute, she screwed up her face and began to cry.

"Jeepers, I knew this would happen," Christine complained from the end of the row. "Give the kid something to suck on, okay? That'll help."

Laura looked around helplessly and Nicki motioned

toward the overhead storage bin. "Her diaper bag's up there, remember? But you'll have to wait until the captain turns off that seat belt sign, or a flight attendant will come along and bite your head off."

"She didn't bite your head off," Meredith remarked reprovingly. "She just wanted you to follow the rules for your own safety."

Rosalind's screaming increased in volume and intensity, and Nicki thought that everyone on the plane must be staring at them. Finally, the plane leveled, the seat belt sign clicked off, and Nicki sprang up and pulled the diaper bag out of the overhead bin.

"Here's a bottle." She grabbed the first container in the bag, untwisted the lid, and handed the bottle to Laura. "Maybe she's hungry, too."

Nicki let the diaper bag fall at her feet and sank back into her seat. They'd been in the air only ten minutes, but with the baby's nonstop crying, it had seemed like an eternity.

"It's working," Laura said when Rosalind stopped crying to drink from her bottle. The baby closed her eyes and slurped rhythmically. "Maybe she'll go to sleep."

Christine unsnapped her seat belt and grabbed the small pillow a flight attendant had placed in her seat. Her red eyes glanced around the cabin. "Sorry, guys," she said, leaning in Nicki's direction. "I don't mean to be a party pooper, but I really don't feel good and there are a couple of empty rows in the back. I'm going to go curl up in one of them and try to sleep."

"Go ahead," Laura said, looking like a little mother with the baby in her arms. "We hope you feel better."

Christine only waved as she made her way toward the back of the plane.

Laura lifted a brow. "Anything else we might need in that diaper bag?" She nodded at Meredith. "Will you look and see? My hands are full."

Meredith sighed and picked up the diaper bag. "Let's see, three disposable diapers," she said, looking through the bag. "Another bottle, this one filled with juice. A bag with crackers, a bag of wipes, and an envelope."

Meredith took the envelope out of the bag. "To whom it may concern," she read.

An internal alarm rang in Nicki's head. "What's that?"

"I don't know." Meredith flipped the envelope over. It wasn't sealed; the flap of the envelope hung open. "Do you think we should read it?"

"The baby concerns us right now," Laura pointed out. "Maybe it's a letter to anyone who might end up baby-sitting her."

"Maybe this letter has nothing to do with the baby," Meredith said, flipping the envelope over again. "But I guess we won't know unless we read it."

"Read it, then," Nicki said.

Meredith pulled a single sheet of white paper from the envelope. A woman's fine hand had written:

To whom it may concern—

Thank you for taking care of my baby, Rosalind. I hope you will forgive me for the unexpectedness of this situation, but I cannot give Rosalind the home she deserves. I hope you will take care of her and see that she is cherished and loved. Please do not let anyone harm her. Tell her I loved her very much. Thank you.

—Rosalind's mother

Four

"I can't believe it!" Nicki stared at Meredith. "Surely that's not right. Rosalind's mother is on the plane, up in row fourteen, just like she said she'd be."

"There's only one way to find out," Meredith said. As Laura sputtered in surprise and shock, Nicki and Meredith left their seats and hurried up the aisle of the plane. In the fourteenth row Nicki recognized a few people she had seen at the airport gate, but the brown-haired woman in the knitted cap was nowhere in sight.

Nicki and Meredith stared at the startled passengers for a moment, then slipped back into their own seats in silence.

"Well?" Laura turned to them with wide eyes. "She's up there, right?"

"No, she's not," Nicki whispered. "Laura, that baby's mother isn't on this plane."

"I don't think she ever intended to be on this plane," Meredith added. "That entire episode at the airport was just her way of getting rid of the baby. She wasn't really sick—she was probably just looking for someone nice and safe to take care of the kid."

"She wouldn't give her baby to just anybody," Nicki added, thinking out loud. "I mean, you wouldn't give it to a strange man or woman, but why not a girl like Laura?"

22

"An American girl," Kim pointed out. "In most other countries, America is considered the land of wealth and opportunity. The mother may have thought Rosalind would have a better chance in America than in Ireland."

"Or wherever she came from." Meredith lifted a finger. "We don't know for sure that baby Rosalind is from Ireland. The woman was in the international concourse at the airport, so she could have flown in from any country in the world."

"What about her accent, Laura?" Kim asked. "Was it Irish? British? American?"

Laura shook her head in confusion. "All I know is she spoke English. You all heard her talk nearly as much as I did—what did you think about her?"

Nicki narrowed her eyes. "Maybe British," she said, struggling to remember what the woman had said. "Or someone who came from somewhere else, but probably not Irish."

"Maybe," Meredith said, "but then again, she could have been disguising her accent so we couldn't trace her. But this is important, Laura—did she tell you her name?"

Laura shook her head again. "I don't remember," she said, her shoulders drooping. "The baby is Rosalind, I remember that, but was her last name McDivit or McDermot? Maybe it was McTrivit, I don't know."

Meredith sank back in her seat. "This is just great. We've had trouble following us ever since we left home. First there was that fiasco in London, then the mystery in Ireland, and now this!"

"It's another mystery," Nicki said, her interest stirring in spite of the cloud of worry that threatened to engulf her. "We've got to find out who this kid belongs to and how we can get her back home."

"If you haven't noticed, we don't have a lot of freedom to investigate," Meredith pointed out. "We're a captive audience here. What can we do on a plane over the Atlantic Ocean? We can't tell the police or access any computer networks—"

"There's one thing we've got to do, and that's tell my mother," Laura said firmly. "Maybe if we can't find the lady, my mom can adopt Rosalind. We ought to at least get first dibs on her."

"First dibs?" Nicki gasped. "I don't think it works like that, Laura. First of all, this baby is a citizen of some country, and that country will want her back."

"Do we have her passport?" Meredith asked. "Is there one in her bag, in her diaper, or maybe in her sweater? The baby had to have a passport to get into the airport gate with her mother."

Nicki searched through the diaper bag. "Nothing in here."

Laura patted the baby's sweater and lifted her frilly dress. "Nothing on the baby."

"Then the mother kept her passport," Meredith said. "She'd have to, because the baby's name, address, and all that stuff would be on the passport. We'd be able to trace her too easily."

"How are we supposed to get her into the United States without a passport?" Nicki looked at Meredith. "We can't lie and say she belongs to one of us. So what do we do?"

Meredith shook her head. "I don't know, but I don't think they'll send her back right away. I suggest we keep things quiet and calm until we land. There's no sense in getting everybody all upset when there's nothing they can do. And in the eight hours that we're flying home, maybe we'll think of some clue or information we've overlooked."

"She's too sweet to be an unwanted baby," Laura whispered, looking down at the little girl in her arms. Rosalind had fallen asleep, her lips curled gently around the nipple of the bottle. Laura covered the baby with her blanket and shifted slightly. "I can't understand it," she whispered again. "Why would anyone want to walk away from such an adorable baby?"

Meredith shook her head. "The world is full of all kinds of people. Even though we may not understand why they do the things they do, most people have a reason. It may sound crazy to us, but it's still a reason."

—

After the flight attendants served soft drinks and peanuts, Nicki stood up to check on Christine. She was awake and sitting four rows back in a double seat, her knees drawn up and covered by a blanket. Nicki could only see the back of Christine's head, because Chris had turned sideways to talk to the girl in the seat behind her.

"Hey, Christine." Nicki moved down the aisle and interrupted their conversation. "You feeling better?"

"A little bit." Christine smiled weakly at Nicki and jerked her thumb toward the girl in the seat behind her. "Nicki, this is Fiona. She's from Dublin and this is her first trip to the United States."

"Hi." Nicki nodded at the striking brown-eyed girl in jeans and a baggy shirt. "It's nice to meet you. Where are you going in the United States?"

"I don't know, really," Fiona answered. "I'll probably stay in Atlanta while I take care of some personal problems. Then I'll see how long I want to travel before I go home again."

What kind of personal problems could this pretty girl could have? Nicki was curious, but she didn't want to pry.

Nicki looked at Christine. "We've got a problem of our own up there. Laura wants her mother to adopt that baby."

Christine yawned, then patted her lips with her hand. "The mother hasn't come for the kid yet? Why not?"

"Because the mother's not on the plane." Nicki nodded with satisfaction when Christine's eyes flew open.

"You mean—" Chris paused as the truth sank in. "Oh boy, what a mess!"

"You said it," Nicki agreed. She nodded again at Fiona. "If Christine drives you crazy with her sniffles, you can come up and talk to us."

"Thanks, but I like being alone," the older girl answered, giving Nicki a crooked half-smile. "I've got some thinking to do."

"We've got a baby you can play with," Nicki offered.

Fiona turned toward the window. "That's the last thing in the world I want to see."

—

When Nicki returned to her seat, Meredith had put away her book and buried her head in a copy of a newspaper from Ireland. "What are you reading?" Nicki asked, slipping quietly into her seat so she wouldn't wake the baby. "Why didn't you ask for an American newspaper?"

"I'm checking the news for reports of missing children," Meredith replied from behind the paper.

Nicki felt her blood run cold. Missing children! Like kids who were snatched—

"Do you think this baby was *kidnapped*?" She pulled the paper away from Meredith's face. "Are we taking someone's baby? Could they get us for being conspirators or something?"

"I don't know," Meredith answered. "But after I thought about it a while, I wondered how a mother could just hand her baby to a stranger and walk away as easily as our lady did. Then I thought, What if she wasn't the kid's mother? Maybe Rosalind is a kidnap victim from some wealthy family. Maybe we're being used to take her far away from the scene of the crime."

When Laura gasped, the baby cried in her sleep. "That can't be," Laura whispered, gently rocking in her seat. "Could it? Oh, please tell me that couldn't be true!"

"That lady in the airport did look young," Nicki said, hoping

Meredith was wrong. "We mentioned it, remember? And she was awfully casual about handing the baby to you, Laura. Could a baby's true mother hand her kid over to strangers like it was no big deal?"

"That's why I'm scanning the paper for news of missing babies." Meredith shook the paper out again. "I'll let you know if I find anything."

Five

A tall, scraggly-faced man in a putty-gray trench coat walked up to the mother who sat on the park bench with her child in her lap. As the mother cooed at her baby, the man reached out and snatched the infant, gathering her into the folds of his coat. When the mother screamed, the stranger slapped her so forcefully that the woman's teeth snapped together with a loud clicking sound. The mother slumped over, her head hitting the park bench with a dull thunk.

The man released a fiendish laugh and clutched the crying baby in a fierce grip as he sped through the park. Waiting for him outside the park gate was the young woman Nicki had seen in the airport rest room. Nicki wanted to cry out, "Stop! Somebody stop them!" but when she drew a breath to scream, her mouth was too dry to even summon a whisper.

Someone gently shook her arm. "I say, young lady, do you want lunch?" Nicki's eyes flew open, and she stared blankly at the young attendant who hovered over her. "Chicken or steak? Which would you prefer?"

"Uh, chicken, please," Nicki stammered, embarrassed she had been caught napping. "Is it time for lunch? It's only ten o'clock."

The handsome young man smiled. "It's three o'clock in the

29

afternoon by Ireland time," he said. "Now, if you'll lower your tray table—"

Nicki fumbled with the tray table on the seat in front of her and lowered it with a clatter. The attendant placed her lunch tray on the table and moved to the next row.

Meredith grinned at Nicki's discomfort. "Caught you by surprise, did he?" She peeled the plastic wrap from her salad plate. "You opened your eyes and stared at him like you had seen a ghost."

"I was dreaming about someone kidnapping the baby," Nicki explained, pulled her silverware from its plastic cover. "That woman I met in the rest room was in my dream, too. I wanted to scream for someone to help, but I couldn't move."

"It's a good thing you couldn't," Meredith answered, smiling. "If you had started screaming here on the plane, you'd have caused a panic. People don't like to be upset on airplanes."

"I guess you're right," Nicki said. She looked over at Laura. Kim had moved over into Christine's empty seat, and baby Rosalind sat between Kim and Laura, held firmly upright by the seat belt. Laura and Kim were eating their lunch and carefully feeding the baby bits of cracker.

"Are you sure she can handle that?" Nicki asked. "She only has two teeth."

"She's getting more on her than in her," Kim said, smiling broadly at the baby. "And these little bits of cracker turn to mush when they've been in her mouth a while."

Nicki turned back to Meredith. "What about the newspaper? Was there any news about a missing baby?"

Meredith shook her head. "Not in the Irish papers. But that doesn't mean she couldn't have been taken in England or Scotland, or even France. I guess she could be from any European Union country."

"You know, I've been thinking." Laura paused to swallow a bite of her steak. "A lot of kids who end up missing in our country are taken by their mothers or fathers after a divorce. What if Rosalind's dad paid that lady we met in the rest room to snatch her from her mother?"

"Or vice versa," Kim said.

"I don't know." Nicki shook her head. "Then where is he? If he wanted custody of the baby, surely that lady wouldn't have given her to us."

"Maybe he backed out of the deal and didn't pay the baby snatcher what he promised," Meredith said, raising a finger. "And she had to get rid of the baby, so she gave her to us."

"There is no way we can keep the baby, so she thought we would give the baby to the authorities," Kim went on, picking up Meredith's thought. "And the baby would be returned eventually to her parents, and the kidnapper would not be caught, and everything would be okay."

"There is one other possibility." Meredith peered at the passengers around her, then lowered her voice and leaned closer to Nicki and Laura. "What if we're part of the plan? Think a minute—what if the baby's father is in the United States and the kidnapping lady needed someone to escort the baby into the country? Maybe after we get off the plane, someone will be waiting to mug us and take the kid—"

"Hush!" Nicki covered her ears. Meredith's idea was too similar to Nicki's nightmare. The thought that her dream might be true was too scary for words.

Laura's smile jelled into an expression of shock. "So whoever's holding the baby when we land could get mugged or something?"

"Do you still want to play the little mother?" Meredith asked.

Laura ran her hand over baby Rosalind's soft hair. "Yes, I do," she whispered. "I don't know how this baby got here or what I'm supposed to do with her, but I'm not dumping her on someone else. And when we land and talk to the police or whoever, I'm not giving her up without a fight."

"I can't picture your mom with a baby," Kim said.

"I don't care." Laura's chin rose. "She won't be my mom's baby, she'll be mine. I'm going to take care of her until we find her true mother, and until we're sure that she's loved and given everything she needs."

"What if her mother doesn't want her?" Meredith pulled the note they had found from her pocket. "What if this note is true? What if the lady in the rest room really was the baby's mother? What if she intends to send the baby to the United States and never see her again?"

"Then we'll find parents who will love her." Laura stabbed her slice of chocolate cake with her fork. "Haven't you ever heard of adoption?"

"Haven't you heard about foster care?" Meredith countered, nearly shouting. "Haven't you heard about kids who spend years in the foster care system waiting for homes?"

"I thought there were lots of people who wanted to adopt." Nicki waved her fork in Meredith's direction. "Why should baby Rosalind have to wait a long time to be adopted?"

"Legalities and red tape," Meredith answered. "Because you can't adopt a baby until the baby's biological parents have signed a paper surrendering their parental rights. And if you can't find those parents, well, no one can adopt her—at least, not right away."

"So not even my mother could adopt Rosalind?" Laura asked.

Meredith shook her head. "It's not as easy as you think," she answered. "And I suggest you stop dreaming about having a baby and start thinking about how we can solve this mystery. There have to be clues somewhere, something we haven't yet thought of."

"What kind of clues can we get from a baby?" Laura snapped. "It's not like she can tell us anything. She can't even talk."

"She can tell us one thing," Kim said, unbuckling the safety belt from around Rosalind's tummy. "I think she's trying to tell us it's time for a diaper change. Laura, you want a baby so much—want to change her diaper?"

Laura went pale, then she made an effort to swallow the food she had been chewing. "Okay," she said, slowly placing her knife and fork into their places on her tray. She glanced toward Nicki. "I don't have any younger brothers or sisters and I've never baby-sat before. What do I do?"

Nicki reached for the diaper bag. "In here is a disposable diaper and a bag of towelettes," she said. "You unfasten the dirty diaper, roll it up, and toss it in the garbage. Then you wipe the baby's bottom with these wet wipes and make sure it's clean. Then you powder her, put a clean diaper under her, and fasten it with the sticky tapes." Nicki pointed toward the tapes on the new diaper.

"Don't goof up," Meredith said, grinning. "We've only got three clean diapers and I'm sure we'll need every one of them before this trip is over."

"I won't mess up." Laura handed her lunch tray to Kim, then lifted the baby. She confidently placed the little girl on her hip, gathered the diaper bag, and raised her chin. "Excuse me, please, Nicki and Meredith, Rosalind and I have something to do."

Nicki laughed as she swiveled to let Laura by. Laura had a good heart, but she had been so spoiled and pampered that some of the simplest things were a challenge for her. "Call if you need help," Nicki said as Laura and the baby moved down the aisle toward the plane's lavatory.

"Thank you, but we can handle a dirty diaper," Laura called over her shoulder, not caring who heard.

Six

Laura didn't come back for fifteen minutes, but Nicki had to admit that when they returned baby Rosalind was happy, clean, and properly diapered. "How did you do?" Nicki asked, amazed that Laura had accomplished her goal without yelling for help.

"Just great," Laura said, then she blushed and giggled. "Okay, so it was harder than I thought. The baby kept wiggling and I couldn't get the diaper around her, but a woman outside knocked on the door and gave me a hand. She was a whiz with a diaper."

Meredith looked around. "Which lady was that?"

"Oh, you'll remember her from the airport," Laura said. "Remember the lady who was talking to my mom? She's the red-haired lady in the pretty skirt. I'm glad she was there when I needed help."

"Speaking of needing help"—Nicki paused to hand her lunch tray to a flight attendant passing by—"has anybody talked to Christine lately? Did she eat lunch?"

"I peeked back at her a little while ago." Kim jerked her thumb in Christine's direction. "She was talking to the girl who's sitting behind her."

"I met her," Nicki said. "Her name's Fiona, and she seems a little strange. She gave me the impression she wants to be left alone."

35

"It's going to be a long flight if she wants to be left alone," Meredith said, standing to stretch her legs. "Especially if she's sitting behind Christine, the human motor mouth." Meredith raised her arms and stretched. "I think I'll take a walk up to first class and talk to your mom, Laura."

"Don't tell her about the baby," Laura begged, her eyes wide. "She'll make me give the baby up right away or something, I know she will. Please, Meredith, don't say anything about Rosalind."

Meredith pulled a package of gum from her jeans pocket. "Okay, I won't say anything," she promised, popping out a rectangle of gum. "But you're going to have to tell her sometime, Laura. She's going to come back here to check on you, so how are you going to hide the baby?"

"I'll think of something," Laura said, beaming down at Rosalind.

"You'd better not lie," Nicki warned. "She'll never trust you if you do."

"I won't lie." Suddenly, Laura snapped her fingers. "Why should my mom come back here to check on me? I'll go up there and save her the trouble. Here, Nicki, will you take the baby while I go with Meredith to see Mom?"

Before Nicki could protest, Laura plopped the baby into Nicki's lap and slid past her into the aisle. "Okay, Meredith, let's go socialize in first class."

Meredith rolled her eyes and followed Laura, while Nicki

looked into baby Rosalind's big blue eyes. "Hey, kiddo," she whispered, watching in fascination as the baby chewed on her fist. "Ba!" Rosalind answered, her cheeks reddening as she grinned up at Nicki.

"Ba yourself," Nicki repeated. Rosalind's eyes widened, then she dimpled and cackled in a surprisingly strong belly laugh.

"Good grief, you laugh like my grandpa," Nicki said, shifting to make more room for Rosalind in her seat.

"Ba da!" Rosalind answered, then she popped her fist into her mouth and resumed chewing and slobbering.

Nicki leaned back against the high cushion of her seat. "At least you smell good now."

When the last lunch tray had been cleared away, the passengers took advantage of the clear aisles to move about the cabin. Nearly every person on board stood to stretch, turned to chat to their neighbor, or walked down the aisle to stand in line at the lavatory. As people of all ages and nationalities passed her, time after time Nicki smiled at people who reached for Rosalind. Most people patted the baby on the head or gently caressed her cheek. Those who didn't reach out to touch Rosalind always smiled and murmured something about how cute and sweet she seemed:

"What a darling baby!"

"Sweet baby, kid. Your sister?"

"What a good traveler you have on your lap, young lady!"

"Oh, seeing that sweet face makes me wish my kids were young again!"

The comments came from right and left, and soon Nicki stopped trying to make pleasant conversation with every person who paused to admire Rosalind. She nodded politely to everyone who said something whether she understood their language or not.

Strangely enough, three people passed Nicki and didn't say a thing about the baby. The first person to ignore Rosalind was the young man in the overcoat and scuffed shoes that Laura had described as a "loser" while they waited in the airport lobby. As he passed on his way to the lavatory, he never even glanced in Nicki's direction, keeping his eyes ahead toward the cockpit of the plane. He never said a word to anyone, not even "excuse me" when he accidentally bumped into a flight attendant.

The second person to ignore Rosalind was the flashy lady in the red suit, the one Nicki had pegged as a television news reporter. She read a *Fortune* magazine as she passed from the first-class section into the coach section, and she never lifted her eyes from the page.

Fiona also ignored Rosalind when she came by, but Nicki wasn't surprised. Nicki felt the older girl's gaze and knew Fiona was watching the baby as she stood in the lavatory line, but when Nicki tried to catch her eye, Fiona looked away. Nicki leaned forward, but Fiona steadfastly refused to acknowledge Nicki and Rosalind, preferring to ignore them altogether.

Seven

"Thank goodness you're back," Nicki blurted when Laura and Meredith made their way back to their seats. "Rosalind's been fussing about something and I don't know how to make her hush."

Laura took Rosalind and jiggled her in her arms, but the change of caregivers did nothing to soothe the fussy child. "She's never cried like this before," Laura said, squeezing past Nicki into her seat. "Do you suppose she's hungry again?"

"I have the other bottle," Kim said, pulling the bottle of apple juice from the diaper bag. "Try this."

Laura put the bottle in Rosalind's mouth, but the baby spat the nipple out, then cried even louder.

"That's not working," Meredith said. "Is there a pacifier in that diaper bag? Something she can chew on?"

"That's a good idea," Nicki said. "She's been chewing on her hand—maybe she's teething."

Rosalind stopped fussing and let out a full-voiced scream. "Good grief, what do I do?" Laura's eyes filled with tears of frustration. "Someone's going to come over here and start asking questions and I have no idea what to do with a screaming baby."

Laura was right. After a minute of the baby's crying, a tall blonde flight attendant approached the girls. "Can I do something to help?" she offered, staring at Laura and Rosalind. "Warm a bottle? Give you a clean diaper?"

"No thanks, she's not hungry." Laura tried to smile through the ear-splitting noise. "I think she's just restless."

"Often the cabin pressure affects babies' ears," the attendant said, opening her hands to Laura. "My name's Bridget, and I'm the head flight attendant. Why don't you let me try holding her?"

Laura didn't hesitate. She handed the baby to Bridget, who held the baby and made soothing clucking sounds. Rosalind quieted almost immediately and soon her ear-shattering screams dissolved into a quiet whimper.

The flight attendant looked over at Laura. "Are you the baby's sister?" she asked. "Where is this child's mother?"

Laura looked at Nicki, and Nicki turned to Meredith. Meredith shook her head.

"Um, we're taking care of the baby for a while," Nicki answered. "The lady who asked us to look after her said she needed to rest because she wasn't feeling well."

Bridget nodded and murmured to the baby, and Nicki glanced at Meredith, surprised that the flight attendant hadn't asked more questions.

"You're a beautiful little girl," Bridget crooned, "and you look an awful lot like my own sweet Katerina."

"You have a baby?" Kim asked. "How old is she?"

"Ten months," the flight attendant answered. "I hate to leave her, but I have to work. I'll be home tomorrow, though."

Baby Rosalind's eyelids began to droop. After a few moments, the flight attendant gently lowered Rosalind into Laura's arms.

"She was tired," the flight attendant said, wiping her hands on her apron. "Babies often get cranky before they fall asleep. If you let her take a nap, she'll be fine, I'm sure."

"Thank you." Laura sighed in relief and gratitude. "You saved us. I had no idea what to do for her."

"If you need anything else, just ask for me," the flight attendant said. "I'd love to help with that beautiful baby." She nodded at Laura. "That baby's mother is getting a bargain with you girls as baby-sitters."

When Bridget walked away, Laura turned to Nicki. "Did you hear that? She thinks I'm a good sitter."

"We'll see how good you are in a couple of hours," Meredith said, pulling a magazine from the seat pocket in front of her. "Just give yourself a little more time."

＊

Nicki knew Christine wasn't asleep. Even though her eyes were closed as she lay curled over two empty seats, Chris tossed and squirmed under the blanket the airline had provided. Nicki reached out and gently touched Christine's arm.

Chris's eyes flew open. "Sorry to bother you." Nicki sank into the empty seat beside her friend. "But since you weren't asleep, I wondered if you felt up to doing something for us."

"I'm not taking care of the baby," Christine croaked, sitting up. "I don't want the baby to get sick."

"No, it's not that," Nicki answered. "It's just that you have really good powers of observation, and I wondered if you'd walk with me through the plane and help me look at the passengers. I'm wondering if maybe that lady who gave us the baby did get on the plane, but somehow she's given us the slip."

Christine lifted a brow. "You mean she's taking advantage of us for free baby-sitting?"

"Maybe, I don't know. But we've been so busy we really haven't looked carefully. Maybe she is on the plane somewhere, maybe wearing a disguise or something."

Christine threw the light blanket off her shoulders. "If I find her, what do I do?"

"Tell her to come take care of her baby." Nicki glanced up to where Laura sat with the sleeping Rosalind in her arms. "If Laura doesn't give that kid up soon, she'll want to keep her, and that's going to cause trouble for everyone."

"And if I don't find this woman?"

"Then we're back where we started," Nicki said simply. "With someone else's baby and no earthly idea what to do with her."

Nicki and Christine walked straight to the front of the plane and paused behind the cockpit door.

Immediately, a flight attendant moved toward them. "Can I help you, girls?"

Nicki elbowed Christine. "We just wanted to stretch our legs."

"I suggest you return to your own cabin."

Nicki nodded, then led the way as she and Chris walked toward the back of the plane. Attendants were careful these days of anyone who got too close to the cockpit. Security was tight on all flights, especially international routes.

Nicki saw several empty seats in the first-class compartment and she recognized several familiar faces among the first-class passengers. Mrs. Cushman sat in her extra-wide seat talking to a white-haired woman with Texas-sized diamonds on her fingers. The flashy lady in the red suit was in first class, too, a tape recorder in one hand and a steno pad in the other. "From Maureen Sullivan to all department heads," she said into a tape recorder as Nicki and Christine approached. "Subject: feature stories. All stories must be approved by my office before expenses are reimbursed on an assignment." Maureen Sullivan raised her head and nodded to Nicki as the girls walked by.

A group of businessmen sat in first class, their briefcases open on their laps, and one long-haired guy sat alone, a copy of *Rolling Stone* on his lap. As he raised his coffee cup to his heavily mustached lips, Christine gripped Nicki's arm. "That's Thad Thumford—the movie star who does all those tough-guy action-adventure films. He's wearing a wig, but I'd recognize him anywhere."

Nicki sneaked another peek at Thad Thumford, but the flight attendant stood behind her, urging her to keep moving toward her own seat.

"Well, our missing mother is definitely not in first class." Christine paused at the curtain that separated the first-class passengers from those who traveled in the coach section. "There's no way any of those people could come close to looking like her."

"Okay, let's look through the next section." Nicki stepped back so Christine could go first down the aisle. The coach section was more crowded than first class, and Nicki felt several people staring at her as she and Christine passed through the compartment.

"Excuse us, we're looking for a friend." Nicki paused to smile at the people who caught her eye. "A lady we met back in the airport."

"Nicki, that's a great idea," Christine whispered. "Let's just make a public announcement." Christine clapped her hands for attention. "Excuse me—we're looking for a friend we met in the airport. She was wearing a knitted cap, a white shirt, and jeans. She has short brown hair and was carrying her baby."

"What's the lady's name?" a woman in the front row asked.

"Um, McDivit, I think," Nicki answered. "But I don't really remember."

Nicki looked around at the group, but no one answered. Several people shook their heads and a few turned away and went back to reading their books or magazines. Nicki felt her heart sink. They were never going to find the mysterious mother this way.

"Don't give up, there are still two more sections," Christine said, pulling Nicki through the cabin. "Come on, we'll look in the next compartment and make another announcement. You never know who'll turn up!"

Eight

Nicki and Christine made their announcement in the next two sections of the plane, but no one answered their questions and no one even came close to resembling the woman who had placed baby Rosalind in Laura's arms. Christine and Nicki walked to the lavatories next and carefully studied every man and woman in line.

"Well, that's it," Christine announced after they had been through the entire plane. "We've looked at every single person on this plane except the pilots, and none of them could be the woman with the baby. And since the flight attendant told us everyone who had a ticket got on the plane, we can assume that our missing mother didn't have a ticket."

"She never intended to get on this plane." Nicki groaned. "I still can't believe it. I was honestly hoping this was all some kind of crazy mistake. I just didn't want to believe any woman would just give up a baby like that."

"At least she didn't leave the baby in a Dumpster," Christine pointed out. "Things like that happen all the time; you can read about them in the newspaper. I read last year that a girl had a baby and tried to drown it—"

"I don't want to hear about it." Nicki covered her ears. "How could anyone do that? I mean, babies are precious! They're little people! But they are so helpless—"

46

"Nicki, I'm really sick," Christine interrupted, clutching her throat. "I think I'm running a fever. If you don't mind, I want to go back to my seat and try to sleep."

Nicki moved out of the aisle so Christine could pass. "Sorry. I really do hope you feel better."

"I will, I guess," Christine mumbled, making her way down the aisle. "But right now I feel as helpless as a baby."

—

Laura grabbed her ear. "Ouch!"

"What's wrong?" Nicki asked as she squeezed in between Meredith's long legs and the seat in front of her.

"Rosalind keeps trying to grab my earrings and she's nearly pulled them out of my ears," Laura complained. "First she pulled my hair, and now she's discovered my earrings. Taking care of this kid can be painful!"

As Laura shifted Rosalind from one shoulder to the other, the baby hiccupped. A stream of formula and juice spattered all over Laura's shirt.

Laura yelped and leaned back. "Oh yuck—I'm covered in baby vomit!"

Nicki bit her lip to keep from laughing as Laura held the baby as far away as she could. Now that her stomach felt better, Rosalind chewed her fist and gurgled.

"Let me take her a while," Kim volunteered.

Laura plopped the baby into Kim's lap.

Nicki laughed. "I thought you wanted to keep her forever,"

she said, wagging her finger at Laura. "What's wrong? Is baby-sitting too much for you?"

"Baby throw-up is too much for anybody," Laura said, standing. "I'll be back as soon as I've cleaned this stuff off."

"Better do a good job," Meredith cautioned. "If you don't want your mom to know about the baby, you'd better not smell like baby spit."

Laura fanned her face and turned to squeeze past Nicki. "Every time I breathe, all I can smell is that sour stuff—"

"So get cleaned up, will you?" Nicki swiveled her legs out of Laura's way. "We don't want to smell that yucky stuff all the way back to Atlanta."

"How many more hours until we get there?" Laura asked, moving past Nicki and Meredith.

"Only six." Meredith winked at Nicki. "We're not even half way home yet."

→

"Uh-oh," Kim said a few moments later. She turned to Nicki. "I feel something wet on my jeans." She lifted baby Rosalind up from her lap, and Meredith, Nicki, and Kim stared at the small wet stain that darkened Kim's jeans.

"Oops." Meredith reached for the diaper bag. "I guess it's time for diaper change number two."

"Kim, you can do the honors this time." Nicki handed a clean diaper to Kim. "Are you up to it?"

"No problem." Kim moved out toward the aisle with the

baby on her hip. "If Laura can manage, I know I can."

After Kim had left, Nicki turned to Meredith. "Any ideas on how we're going to solve this mystery?" Nicki asked. "I don't see how we're going to have time to do any investigating. The baby is keeping us too busy."

"Now I know what my mother went through when she took time off to raise us kids," Meredith said. "I read the other day that the average housewife walks ten miles a day around the house doing her chores. She'll spend twenty-five hours a year just making beds."

"How many hours will she spend changing diapers?" Nicki asked. "And how many diapers will she change?"

Meredith shook her head. "I don't know, but I could probably figure it out if you really want me to."

"Never mind," Nicki said, spying Laura in the aisle. "Here comes Laura, and I don't think she'll want to hear about this. Maybe we should change the subject."

Meredith waited until Laura had stepped into their crowded row, then she smiled. "Did everything come out, Laura? I would imagine that baby puke would be hard to get out of a shirt. I read in my book of fabulous factoids that the human sense of smell is so keen that it can detect the odors of certain substances even when they are diluted to one part to thirty billion."

Laura frowned. "If that's your way of telling me I still stink, Meredith, it's not very nice," she said, moving back out toward the aisle of the plane. "Okay, I'll go wash up again, but I'll probably catch pneumonia from sitting in a wet shirt on an air-conditioned plane. And it'll be all your fault!"

As Laura stomped toward the lavatory, Meredith turned to Nicki. "Can't she take a joke?" she asked, frowning.

"Never mind." Nicki settled back into her seat. "We're all a little nervous right now."

Nine

The in-flight movie had just begun when Kim returned with the baby. Nicki adjusted her earphones so she could hear the audio portion of the film. The lights went down in the cabin and the passengers in window seats pulled down the blinds to make the cabin nice and dark. Nicki hoped Rosalind would take the hint and go to sleep. The baby, however, had other ideas.

"Ouch, she's trying to yank the earphones out of my ears," Kim complained, handing the baby to Nicki. "Why don't you take her a while?"

Rosalind's eyes glinted with mischief, so Nicki passed her to Meredith. "You haven't had a turn with the kid yet, have you?" Nicki asked, pulling the diaper bag with her foot. "Why don't you baby-sit for a while? I want to watch the movie."

"Great," Meredith said, giving up and letting Rosalind have her plastic earphones. "I didn't want to watch this movie anyway."

The movie was *Thank Heaven for Little Girls*, a film about two-year-old triplets who were left on the doorstep of a convent. Nicki giggled as the little kids created mayhem in the nuns' lives, then she stopped laughing. Rosalind's situation was uncomfortably similar, but it was real life, not a movie. There wasn't anything humorous about being stuck with a stranger's baby on a transatlantic flight.

Nicki removed her earphones and watched Meredith. Meredith had cuddled Rosalind close in her arms and was whispering to the baby. "You might think cellophane is made of plastic, Rosalind, but it is not," Meredith read in a sing-song voice from *222 Fabulous Factoids*. "It is made from a plant fiber called cellulose, which has been shredded and aged. Cellophane was invented in 1908 by a Swiss chemist named Jacques Brandenberger who was trying to make a stain-proof tablecloth and ended up with cellophane instead."

"Good grief," Nicki interrupted, laughing. "What are you telling her?"

Meredith shrugged. "I happen to think it's a colossal waste of time to sit around saying ga-ga and goo-goo to babies. They can understand more than you think they can."

"I wonder if Rosalind understands that she's away from her mother," Nicki whispered. "I wonder if she misses her."

"You know, I've been thinking about that," Meredith said. A woman in the row in front of them turned around and gently laid a finger across her lips, so Meredith lowered her voice.

"There are two Bible stories about babies that might give us insight into this situation," Meredith continued, settling Rosalind in a more comfortable position on her lap. "The first one I thought of was the time Solomon was confronted with two mothers and one baby. Remember that story?"

"The mothers were each claiming the child," Nicki said,

remembering the story. "Solomon said they should cut the child in half."

"That's right," Meredith said. "The false mother didn't care, but the child's real mother fell to her knees and begged for mercy. She said she was willing to give the child to the other woman rather than see it die under the sword."

Nicki wrinkled her nose. "How does that help us? We don't have two mothers here—we don't have *any* mothers."

"That brings me to the second story." Meredith wriggled her fingers and Rosalind giggled. "Remember when the pharaoh of Egypt decreed that all the Hebrew boy babies were to be thrown into the Nile? One lady hid her son for three months, then made a basket of reeds and put her baby in the river."

"Moses." Nicki snapped her fingers. "I remember making tiny baskets in Sunday school when I was a little kid. We drew faces on clothespins and put them in the baskets—they were supposed to be Moses."

Meredith raised her eyebrows. "Whatever. Anyway, the mother abandoned her baby because she knew she had to, but what else did she do?"

Nicki thought a minute. "I don't remember," she confessed. "Did she send a month's supply of diapers or write a note? What are you getting at, Meredith?"

"She sent a guardian," Meredith said. "Moses' older sister was sent to the river to keep an eye on the basket in the reeds.

Moses' mother didn't want any crocodiles or anything tipping over that basket."

"Oh yeah, a guardian," Nicki echoed. She glanced around, then leaned close to Meredith's ear. "Do you think there's a guardian on this plane for baby Rosalind?"

"I think a mother who loves her child will do anything to make sure that child is not harmed," Meredith said. "Just like the mother who faced Solomon. Just like Moses' mother."

Nicki crooked her index finger in front of Rosalind's blue eyes. Rosalind eagerly grabbed Nicki's finger and laughed. "How do we know Rosalind's mother really loves her?" Nicki said slowly. "Maybe she's not like those other mothers."

"I think she is," Meredith said. "Just look at this kid—she's happy, she's well fed, and someone obviously stocked her diaper bag with enough stuff to get her through this trip. I think Rosalind's mother loves her very much."

"She wouldn't just hand us her kid and walk away," Nicki said, thinking of how casually the woman in the airport had behaved.

"No, she wouldn't," Meredith agreed. "That's why I'm sure the woman who gave us this baby wasn't Rosalind's mother. Maybe Rosalind's mother couldn't afford to feed the baby, or maybe she's dying from cancer or something, so she asked someone to help her find a good home for Rosalind."

"So the friend took the baby to the airport and put her on a plane bound for the United States . . ."

"And to be sure the baby arrived safely, she sent a guardian." Meredith nodded firmly. "Of course, I could be wrong, but if I loved my baby and couldn't take care of her, I'd be careful to make sure my plan for her wouldn't fail. I wouldn't send her to America unless someone was keeping an eye on her."

"We're keeping an eye on her."

Meredith rolled her eyes. "I mean a responsible adult. I wouldn't send my baby off with five teenage girls."

Nicki sighed. "I guess we're not responsible adults."

"No, but we were a brilliant way to put the baby on the plane without arousing attention," Meredith answered. "No adult would be dumb enough to take a baby like we did."

"So we're being used," Nicki said, summing up the situation. "We were used to bring the baby on the plane—"

"Without a ticket," Meredith added. "Babies fly cheaper than adults, but there's still a charge on overseas flights. Rosalind is flying free, and without a passport."

"And we didn't think of any of that," Nicki said.

"Didn't think of what?" Laura interrupted, coming back to her seat from the rest room. Laura's shirt was clean, but covered in wet blotches. Laura frowned when she saw the baby in Meredith's arms.

"Do you want to take the baby for a while?" Meredith asked.

"No, thanks," Laura said, sliding past Meredith and Nicki to her seat. "You can keep her." She fell into her seat and sighed. "Now what are y'all talking about? What didn't we think of?"

"Passports and airline tickets," Nicki said. "Meredith thinks maybe there's a guardian on this plane—you know, someone to watch over Rosalind and make sure she gets to Atlanta safe and sound."

"That's crazy," Laura said. "If someone wants to make sure the baby gets to Atlanta, why doesn't this mysterious someone just take her there?"

"I don't have all the answers—yet," Meredith said, bouncing Rosalind on her knee. "But I'll bet if we took the baby through the plane, someone might drop a hint or give themselves away."

"If the guardian thought the baby was in danger, he or she would have to come out of hiding," Nicki whispered, excitement rising in her voice.

"I'm not going to let you do anything dangerous with her," Laura snapped. "Even though I am kinda mad at the kid for puking on me, I'm not going to let you hang her out the window or anything."

"How about sickness?" Meredith asked. "Maybe if the guardian thought the baby was sick—we're just kids, we don't know anything about how to care for a sick baby. The guardian would have to step forward to help."

"But the baby's not sick," Laura protested. "She's the happiest, healthiest-looking kid I've ever seen."

"She'll be hungry soon," Nicki whispered. "And when she is, she'll cry. And when she cries, she'll look sick." Nicki nodded firmly. "Trust me. When my little brother and sister get crabby, the first thing my mother does is feel their foreheads to see if they have a fever. They're usually just hungry."

"Okay, then, we'll canvass the cabin when the baby starts to cry for dinner," Meredith said, passing the baby to Nicki's lap. "Here, Nicki, it's your turn. Entertain our guest for a while, will you?"

Meredith reclined her chair and closed her eyes, and Nicki looked at the squirming bundle on her lap. *Maybe there is something you can tell us.* Nicki looked at the baby's rosy cheeks. *Maybe you know the guardian, and maybe you'll reach out to him or her and tell us what we need to know.*

Rosalind's head swiveled in the direction of the movie screen, and the antics of the two-year-old triplets caught her eye. Nicki smiled and turned Rosalind so she could watch the flickering images on the screen. Entertaining a baby wasn't so hard.

Ten

Nicki glanced at her watch and sighed. At home, her parents, Sarah, and Josh had finished lunch and were probably out playing in the yard or relaxing with a video game. They wouldn't get ready to drive to the airport for hours yet. Did her family miss her at all?

As a wave of homesickness swept over her, she hugged Rosalind so tightly that the baby squealed in protest. "Oh, hush, you're okay," Nicki whispered. "You're fine and we'll find someone to take care of you before the day's over, I promise."

"Five hours till Atlanta," Meredith said, checking her watch. "We'll be in Atlanta by five thirty and Tampa by eight thirty. Just think, we'll be in our own beds by nine tonight."

"I can't wait to be in my own bed," Nicki answered, "but we've only got five hours to find Rosalind's guardian." She scooped Rosalind up in her arms and handed the baby to Laura. "Here, Laura, it's your turn. I've got to walk around and stretch my legs. I don't remember the flight to England taking this long."

"We slept through most of that flight," Kim pointed out. "Now we're awake."

"I wish I wasn't," Nicki grumbled, standing and squeezing past Meredith in the narrow row. "I wish I could close my eyes and wake up in my own bed."

Nicki glanced back toward the seat where Christine had been seated, but there was no sign of Christine's red head. Nicki hurried down the aisle and found her friend curled up in her seat, a navy blue blanket thrown over her shoulders.

Fiona, the dark-haired girl behind Christine, caught Nicki's eye, so Nicki gestured toward Christine. "Is she okay?" she whispered. "Did she finally fall asleep?"

"She was running a little fever, so I gave her a couple of aspirin. She's been asleep for about half an hour," Fiona answered. "And what a relief! For someone who doesn't feel good, that girl sure can talk!"

"Christine could talk the wings off a fly," Nicki answered, smiling broadly.

"She told me about that baby you have up there," Fiona went on, a wounded look in her dark eyes. "What are you going to do with her? You're not going to keep her, are you?"

"We can't, she's not our baby," Nicki said. A sudden idea struck Nicki's imagination—was it possible that this girl was Rosalind's mother? Nicki had no idea how old Fiona was, but teenagers had babies every day, didn't they?

"We think her mother is somewhere close by," Nicki answered. "And we really want to help make sure the baby is reunited with her mom. She's such a sweet little girl and I'm sure her mother must love her very much."

"Not me, I hate kids," Fiona blurted out.

Nicki swallowed hard. "Why do you hate kids?" Nicki sank

into the empty seat next to Fiona. "You were a kid once, you know."

"Aren't you insightful?" Fiona turned away from Nicki and looked out the window. "I don't know why I hate kids, I just do," she said finally. "They're so much trouble! Your life is going along just fine, and then, blam! You're pregnant, you throw up all the time, you go through the most painful experience of your life, and for what? For a little person who screams day and night for your constant attention, and your life goes on hold for the next twenty years while you raise an ungrateful, spoiled brat! Do I want that kind of misery? No thank you, I do not!"

Nicki managed a little laugh. "I'm sure it's not that bad," she said. "If raising children is really that bad, then why do people have babies all the time? My mother loves kids, and Christine's mother really loves them. The Kelshaws have six kids at home, and I wouldn't be surprised if they have more one day."

"No wonder that girl's so daft," Fiona said, forcing a laugh. "But I know how she feels. Me parents are Catholic, and we've got seven kids still in our house. I jumped at the chance to go to the United States just to get away from home. I have an older sister in Atlanta, and I'm going to spend some time there on holiday while I work some things out."

Nicki sighed in disappointment. If Fiona was telling the truth, she wasn't Rosalind's mother. She was just what she said—an Irish girl taking her vacation in the United States.

"Well, if you think of anything that could help us with this baby, we'd appreciate it," Nicki said, standing. "We've been racking our brains to think of clues we could use to reunite baby Rosalind with her mother and father."

"Now what would I know about that baby?" Fiona snorted. "Leave her be, that's what I'd do. Just hand her over to someone at the airport and be on your way. You're too young to live your life for someone else."

Nicki shook her head and moved away. Back at her seat, baby Rosalind had begun to cry in earnest. It had to be time for the baby's dinner.

•

"Okay, this is it," Meredith said, lifting the baby into her arms. "We go through the plane with our crying baby and tell people who look interested that we think she's sick."

"If the guardian is on board, he or she should do something," Nicki said, grabbing the diaper bag. "But we can only do this for about five minutes, Meredith. I can't stand here and listen to her cry when I know she's hungry and just wants a bottle."

"It's for her own good," Meredith answered. "Now, grab that diaper bag and come on."

They began a slow walk through the plane with Rosalind, who protested with all her might. Soon tears were running down the baby's cheeks, and the sight of those tears brought more than one passenger to her aid.

Bridget, the flight attendant, rushed forward. "Oh, what's

wrong with our youngest passenger?" she crooned, holding out her hands for the baby. "Can I do something?"

"We think she may be sick," Nicki said, standing between Meredith and Bridget. "What do you think?"

"She's probably starving," Bridget answered. "Can I warm a bottle for you?"

"No thanks, she doesn't like hot apple juice," Meredith answered, moving quickly down the aisle.

In the next section Nicki recognized Megan O'Connor, the short, red-haired woman who had talked to Mrs. Cushman in the airport lobby. "That darling child," Mrs. O'Connor exclaimed, her eyes wide with concern. "Is something wrong?"

"We think she may be sick," Nicki said, watching as the woman stood and put her hand on the baby's forehead.

"This child isn't sick, she's hungry," Mrs. O'Connor answered firmly. "You must feed her at once, or call the flight attendant for help."

"Thanks, we will," Nicki said, moving on toward the front of the plane.

At the curtained opening, Meredith stopped abruptly. "Mrs. Cushman is in first class," Meredith whispered. "How do we explain this?"

Nicki pulled Meredith back into the coach section. "We don't even go in there," she said. "I don't think Rosalind's mother is the type to fly first class. Besides, we know Mrs. Cushman isn't

Rosalind's mother, and the only other middle-aged woman in there is Maureen Sullivan, that businesswoman in the red suit."

"I suppose you have a point." Meredith turned away from the curtained entry. "If someone wanted to be a guardian for Rosalind, they wouldn't hide themselves away in the first-class section. They'd want to sit where they could keep an eye on her."

"So let's feed this kid," Nicki said. "Maybe Operation Baby Tears wasn't such a good idea."

Eleven

The three darling triplets were still giving the nuns trouble on the screen in the front of the plane as Nicki settled into her seat. Beside her, baby Rosalind sucked greedily on the bottle of apple juice in Laura's arms. Apparently, Laura had forgiven Rosalind for the humiliation she felt when Rosalind spit up on her.

"Well, I know one person who's definitely not Rosalind's guardian," Nicki whispered to Meredith. "That Fiona girl sitting behind Christine. She absolutely despises kids. I have the feeling she could throw every kid on this plane out the window and feel good about doing it."

"She couldn't be that bad," Meredith answered, putting down *222 Fabulous Factoids*. "I can't believe that anyone could really hate babies. They're too cute." Meredith cocked her head. "Speaking of babies, did you know a newborn baby's head accounts for about one-quarter of its entire weight?"

Nicki rolled her eyes. "Stick to important things, Meredith. We're trying to find someone on this plane who might be here to watch the baby."

"I suppose we could just walk through the plane and ask everyone if they know her or anything about her," Nicki said, shrugging. "At this point, what do we have to lose? If the guardian wants to remain hidden, he or she just won't say anything."

"Nicki!" Kim's agonized whisper cut through the silence of the cabin.

Nicki leaned over Laura and the baby. "What?"

"I just thought of something," Kim answered. "What if there's a guardian for Rosalind and she was kidnapped? What if one of the kidnappers is on the plane to make sure we don't run to the police or something?"

Nicki turned back to Meredith. "What about that theory?" She sank low in her seat. "What if the baby's guardian isn't a good guy—what if some bad guys are on the plane just to make sure the baby is—disposed of?"

Meredith scowled. "That's a disgusting thought," she said. "What would they do, jump us once we got off the plane? There's no other way they could keep us from going to the authorities, so if they want to see her gone—"

"Maybe sending her to the United States is just their way of getting her out of the picture," Nicki said. "But maybe there's a kidnapper on board, and it's his job to make sure the baby doesn't come back to Ireland."

"Or maybe it's his job to make sure the baby does go back to Ireland," Kim pointed out. "What if the baby was snatched in England or Germany or France? If she's found on a plane from Ireland, that's where the American authorities will send her, and it'll take so much time the kidnappers will be able to get the ransom money and get away."

Laura chewed on her thumbnail. "I don't want to hear any

more about any of this kidnapping stuff," she snapped, taking the empty bottle out of Rosalind's mouth. "You'll upset the baby." She tilted her head and smiled at Rosalind. "Was that good?" she crooned. "I can't believe they made you wait for your afternoon snack."

"Don't forget to burp her," Nicki said, elbowing Laura. "You put her on your shoulder and pat her back until she burps."

"Disgusting!" Laura frowned. "Why would I want to do that?"

"It will remove the air bubbles from her stomach, anyone knows that," Meredith answered. "Here, pass her to me. I'll burp her if you don't want to."

"You can have her," Laura said, passing the baby over Nicki's lap to Meredith. "I don't want her spitting up on me again."

Baby Rosalind grinned playfully and grabbed at a strand of Meredith's dark hair. "Careful, kid, that's connected to my head," Meredith said, turning to look the baby in the eye. "But healthy hair can stretch 25 percent of its length without breaking."

"What's she talking about?" Laura asked Nicki.

"It's a fabulous factoid," Nicki answered, shaking her head. "From Meredith's latest book. I guess we'll just have to put up with it for a while."

"Not me," Laura said, slipping the earphones over her head. "This dumb movie is bound to be better than listening to fascinating factagrams."

"Factoids," Nicki whispered, knowing Laura couldn't hear. She turned back to Meredith. "I guess we shouldn't go through the plane and ask people about the baby. We really don't have any way of knowing if the baby's guardian is here to protect her—"

"Or to keep her away from her parents," Meredith said finishing Nicki's thought. "You're right. But we've got to do something."

—

With her movie headphones still on, Kim leaned against Laura's chair and slept. Laura watched the film in silent concentration, and Meredith had again picked up her copy of *222 Fabulous Factoids*. Baby Rosalind sat in Nicki's lap squirming in frustration. "I don't know what to do with you, so please don't cry," Nicki said, lowering her head to the baby's level. "Do you want to walk around? Let's take a walk."

Nicki leaned the baby against her shoulder and squeezed past Meredith into the aisle. A long line of people waiting for the lavatory blocked the way in front of her, so she turned and walked toward the back of the plane. Nicki was glad to see Christine awake and looking out the window.

"Are you feeling better?" Nicki asked, standing in the aisle in front of Christine. "You look like you've been asleep for five years."

"I know." Christine smoothed her tousled hair with one hand. "I felt like I was dying an hour ago, but I feel better now. Do you think they'll feed us again? Now I'm hungry."

"They'll probably bring peanuts around in a little while," Nicki said, grinning. "Or maybe pretzels."

Fiona glanced up at Nicki and the baby. " I see you've still got your little side show."

"If you mean the baby, of course we've still got her," Nicki replied, ignoring the sharp edge in Fiona's voice. "She's adorable." An idea struck Nicki and she walked closer to Fiona. "Would you like to hold Rosalind for a while?"

Fiona drew back as if Nicki had offered her a poisonous snake. "No way." She threw her hands up in a defensive gesture. "Don't get me stuck with that kid. How do I know you won't just walk off and leave me like the kid's mother did? A lot of people walk off, you know."

"We're not going to leave her until we're sure she's in good hands," Nicki replied. "We want to try to find her parents. I'm not sure exactly how we're going to do it, but we're going to protect this baby."

Twelve

"That baby's mother obviously didn't want her," Fiona said, turning her face to the window. "She'd be better off if she had never been born. If I had a kid I didn't want, I wouldn't want to spend the rest of my life worrying about her."

Nicki gasped. "That's crazy," she said, sinking into the seat next to Fiona. "Do you honestly mean that you'd rather see this beautiful little girl dead than taken in by adoptive parents? How can you mean that?"

Fiona turned toward Rosalind and Nicki. "I'll bet you're one of those people who protest in front of abortion clinics," she said, her words edged with bitterness. "I've read about such protests in the United States. Those people parade about, destroying the peace and denying women their constitutional rights to an abortion, yet where are those people when unwanted babies need help? Where are they when single mothers need money?"

Christine turned in her seat and faced Fiona. "My mom and dad have led abortion protests," she said, her voice firm and strong despite her sickness. "They help support a home for teenage mothers in our town, and two of my brothers are adopted. In my family, we do put our actions behind our beliefs."

"Well, others don't," Fiona countered. "What about the law? People like your parents are taking away women's freedom—"

"Freedom?" Nicki asked. "How so? They don't stop anyone from going into an abortion clinic. They just want to talk to the women and tell them about other choices."

"They're taking away the right of choice," Fiona answered. "We don't have the right to choose abortion in Ireland, but you do in the United States."

"Those women and girls have choices all right," Christine answered. "They have the choice not to have sex in the first place. They have the choice to use self-control. They have the choice of saying no. Trouble is, they say yes to all the wrong things and expect an abortion to solve all their problems. It won't."

"But the American Constitution guarantees—"

"It doesn't say anything about the right to an abortion," Nicki said. "It says that all people have the right to life, liberty, and the pursuit of happiness. All people. That means big people and little people, born people and unborn people. Take Rosalind and me—do I have more rights than she does?"

Fiona scowled. "What are you talking about?"

Nicki patted the baby's back. "Do I have more rights than Rosalind just because I'm bigger than she is?"

"Of course not," Fiona admitted. "You're both people. Age doesn't make any difference in the eyes of the law."

"That's right," Nicki said, nodding confidently. "Age doesn't make any difference, and size doesn't, either. The law protects us equally, as it should also protect people who are unborn.

Just because they're younger and smaller doesn't mean we should be able to abort them."

"Call it what it is," Christine said. "Abortion is killing." Her eyes began to water. "A friend of my sister's had an abortion and told us about it. She said the people at the abortion clinic lied to her. They told her it wasn't a baby, that it was just a fetus, a clump of tissue, so she had an abortion and didn't even tell her parents. But the nurse slipped up and the girl had a look at what they were carrying out of the room, and she saw her baby's arms and legs—"

Christine's voice broke and a tear trickled down her cheek.

"I think what Christine's trying to say is that her friend's baby died that day," Nicki said, holding Rosalind near her heart. "What they call a fetus is a baby. I read in a book that a baby's heart starts beating two and a half weeks after a woman's egg is fertilized. His brain begins to work at six weeks. At two months, before a pregnant woman is even showing, unborn babies have complete, tiny bodies. They can grab their fingers and toes, swim, hiccup, suck their thumbs, and go to sleep."

"And most abortions take place around three months," Christine added, wiping tears from her face. "But in some states it's perfectly legal to kill unborn babies even up to the day of delivery."

Nicki couldn't stop a shiver. "It makes you wonder, doesn't it, about how close people could come to actually killing babies who were born and not wanted?" she asked. "I mean, if we can legally kill babies that are only hours away from being born, what's to stop people from legally killing babies who have been born only a few hours?"

Fiona sniffed. "The law protects them, you idiots."

"The law should protect everybody," Christine said, shaking her finger in Fiona's face. "But it doesn't."

"What's this about?"

Nicki looked up. Meredith had left her copy of 222 *Fabulous Factoids* on her seat and had come back to join the conversation.

"Did we bother you?" Nicki asked, feeling her cheeks redden. "Were we that loud?"

"Let's just say that everyone in this section of the plane now knows what you and Christine believe about babies," Meredith said, sinking into the empty seat next to Christine. She turned to face Nicki. "So what brought all this on?"

Nicki nodded at Fiona, who sat with her arms folded. "Fiona just said she thought Rosalind would be better off unborn than unwanted. We disagreed."

"You know, there used to be people in America who didn't think much of slaves." Meredith spoke softly. "Killing a slave was not a serious crime, because, after all, a slave was nothing but property. Negro slaves didn't have constitutional rights. They didn't have freedom."

"What's slavery got to do with anything?" Fiona's dark eyes flashed at Meredith. "A woman's right to abortion has nothing to do with slavery."

"It's the point I'm trying to make," Meredith answered patiently. "My ancestors were slaves in America, and this point means a lot to me. You see, in 1857 the U.S. Supreme Court ruled in the Dred Scott decision that slaves had no rights and could not be citizens of the United States."

"Until the Civil War," Nicki inserted. "Then Abraham Lincoln freed the slaves—"

"—and the thirteenth, fourteenth, and fifteenth amendments to the Constitution guaranteed our rights as citizens," Meredith went on. "Well, in 1973, when the Supreme Court ruled that states could not prevent women from having abortions, they effectively stripped unborn Americans of their right to life, liberty, and freedom. Abortion does the same thing that slavery did. Under current laws, unborn babies have no rights as citizens, and that's not right."

"But a fetus is not alive," Fiona argued.

"Of course it is," Christine blurted out. "It lives, swims, and breathes—what more do you want?"

"But a fetus can't live outside the mother's body," Fiona snapped. "It's nothing but a parasite."

"You couldn't live long without food, water, or shelter, either," Meredith answered. "All of us could be considered parasites, in a way. None of us is completely independent."

"You can't tell when life really begins," Fiona said hopelessly, waving her hands as if to wave Nicki, Christine, and Meredith away. "I don't want to talk about this anymore."

Nicki responded, "Life doesn't begin, it is passed on as a gift." The baby snored softly, and Fiona's lip quivered.

"The mother's egg and the father's sperm are alive, just like your fingers and toes are alive," Nicki explained. "Life began a long time ago, when God created man, and life is passed on from mother and father to children. That has been God's plan from the beginning. You can't say that a baby is not alive one minute and suddenly alive the next. Every cell in its body is alive from the beginning."

Fiona turned her back to Nicki. "Please leave."

Nicki stood up slowly so she wouldn't wake the baby. "Okay," she said, motioning for Meredith to follow her. "Christine, I hope you feel better."

"I feel better already," Christine answered, curling up into a ball in her seat. "I love a good discussion."

Thirteen

2:00 PM Eastern Standard Time

"I'm hungry," Laura announced, looking around. "It's been hours since we ate."

"I'm sure they'll bring us a snack soon," Nicki said, smiling at Rosalind. The baby blinked her blue eyes and smiled. "I think Rosalind's hungry, too."

"Speaking of food," Meredith interrupted, reading from her book, "did you know that there is about one-tenth of a calorie's worth of glue on every postage stamp?"

"I didn't know that," Nicki whispered, watching Rosalind reach for Meredith's colorful book. "But I know we're out of food in the diaper bag. What will we do when Rosalind starts to cry?"

"I'd worry more about her diaper supply," Laura said, reaching under the seat for the diaper bag. She pulled out the only remaining diaper. "This is her last chance to stay clean and dry."

"She is wet," Nicki said, feeling the thickness of Rosalind's diaper. "I guess I'd better go change her. That is, unless one of you wants to do it?"

Laura turned away rapidly, and Meredith scowled. Even sweet Kim grinned at Nicki and shook her head. "It's your turn, Nicki." Kim held her nose. "Good luck!"

"It's no big deal," Nicki said, standing with the baby. "I've changed lots of diapers. I've just never done it in such a tiny bathroom."

The line for the lavatory was not as long as it had been after lunch, and Nicki welcomed the chance to stretch her legs and look around. People were growing restless on the long flight. The movie was over, the lights had been turned on, and several men and women were pacing aimlessly up and down the aisle. One man flipped furiously through a magazine, a stack of others in the aisle by his seat.

In the narrow galley that served as the airplane's kitchen, several flight attendants were bustling about preparing the late-afternoon snack. "Are we eating again?" Nicki asked as she moved past the galley.

A startled flight attendant looked up. "Oh, just soup and sandwiches," she answered, her hands deftly replacing foil covers on bowls of steaming soup. "Cream of tomato soup and chicken salad sandwiches with crackers and cheese."

Bridget, the tall blonde flight attendant, walked up with a box in her hands. "I believe this must be for you," she said, offering the small cardboard container to Nicki. "You're holding the only baby on this flight."

"What?" Nicki jiggled the squirming baby and looked at the box. It was of plain brown cardboard, taped shut, and about the size of Nicki's little brother's lunch box. Someone had penciled "For the baby" on the outside.

Nicki carefully took the box in her free hand. "Thank you," she said, resting the baby on her hip. "I wonder what it could be."

Bridget smiled. "You never know," she said, moving back

down the aisle. "Sometimes people just take a fancy to you, and leave little presents. Enjoy it."

"Ba-ba-ba-da," Rosalind said, tapping the box with her fist. She lowered her head as if she would bite the box, and Nicki laughed and moved it out of her reach.

"No, we don't eat everything," Nicki chided gently, jiggling Rosalind. "Only food, okay? And soon you'll have some crackers to chew on." The lavatory line moved forward and Nicki took a step. "I wonder," she said, gazing into Rosalind's deep blue eyes. "Can you drink cream of tomato soup in a bottle?"

Nicki didn't open the box in the lavatory because Rosalind kept her too busy. There was no counter to support the baby, so Nicki had to sit on the toilet, place the baby in her lap, and change Rosalind's diaper as the baby wriggled and swiveled her head to see everything.

"We'll let Auntie Meredith open your present for you," Nicki told Rosalind as they slipped out through the narrow lavatory door. "Maybe it's something you can play with."

Laura, Meredith, and Kim were fascinated with Nicki's story about the box. "What do you think is in it?" Kim asked, her dark eyes wide with curiosity. "A gift?"

"Could be," Nicki said, shrugging. "Why don't we open it and find out?"

"Wait a minute," Meredith cautioned, holding the box at

arm's length. "What if it's something dangerous? What if this is from the kidnappers?"

"It won't hurt us," Nicki said. "A bomb would never have made it through security. I think you should open it."

Meredith nodded in agreement, then she used her long thumbnail to slit the tape at the seams of the box. She lifted the lid open and gasped.

"What is it?" Kim asked, leaning over Laura.

"A present?" Laura asked, peering past Nicki. "Anything expensive?"

Nicki pulled away from the box. "Something bad?"

"Something great," Meredith answered She put her hand in the box and lifted out three disposable diapers, a baby spoon, a bottle of grape juice, a jar of strained peaches, and a box of soft crackers.

Laura frowned. "I wouldn't call that stuff great."

"We needed these things," Nicki said, taking the spoon and the jar of peaches from Meredith. "Rosalind's hungry."

"This proves my theory," Meredith said, scanning the cabin for anyone who might be watching the girls. "There is a guardian on board this plane. Someone packed extra stuff for the baby and sent it to us just when we needed it. Someone's watching us and making sure Rosalind has everything she needs."

"It'll be easy enough to find the guardian now," Nicki said, grinning. "All we have to do is ask Bridget who gave her the box. It's a cinch."

Laura reached up and pressed the overhead button that summoned an attendant. Within seconds, Bridget appeared at the end of their aisle. "Do you need something?" she asked, smiling down at the girls. Rosalind's eyes brightened as she reached out for Bridget.

Nicki opened the jar of peaches. "We wanted to thank whoever gave you the box for the baby. Can you tell us who it was?"

Bridget shook her head. "I'm sorry, girls, but no one gave me the box. We found it on the floor of the back galley. I have no idea who put it there."

Nicki sighed in disappointment. Why was the guardian taking such pains to remain hidden? And why couldn't they fit the pieces of the puzzle together? They had been so close, but now the girls were completely without a clue—again.

"When did you find the box?" Meredith asked.

Bridget shrugged. "We found it when we went back there to prepare the afternoon snack," she explained. "I suppose it could have been left there at any time during the afternoon."

Nicki spooned peaches into Rosalind's tiny gaping mouth. The baby smacked her lips greedily and opened her mouth for more. "As you can see, the baby obviously loves peaches," Nicki said. "Whoever left that box for her sure knew what she was doing."

Bridget paused. "When I have a moment, I want you to tell me all about this baby," Bridget said, giving the girls a curious look. "But it will have to wait. I've got to go serve now."

She hustled off toward the rear section of the plane, and Nicki turned to Meredith. "Well, so much for solving the mystery," she said. "We're back where we started."

"Not really," Meredith said. "Did you notice that the baby liked Bridget? It was almost like Rosalind knows her."

"Yeah." Laura laughed. "Maybe the baby is Bridget's and all this is just her way of taking her baby to work. She flies across the ocean with free baby-sitters, then she claims the baby and flies home again."

"She did mention that she had a baby girl," Nicki said, recalling her earlier conversation with the flight attendant. "Could she be the one who put this box together for us?"

"It's crazy, but it's possible," Meredith said. "Maybe whoever takes care of her baby got sick or something. So Bridget gives the baby to a friend, who gives her to us. We take care of her on the flight, then Bridget claims her when we arrive in Atlanta."

"Better yet, she listens to our story and tells us to give the baby to her when we land," Kim said, snapping her fingers. "After all, she is the head flight attendant, right? It would be natural for us to give the baby to her."

"And she'll tell us that without a passport, the baby has to be returned to Ireland," Meredith summed up, her eyes sparkling. "So Bridget flies back to Ireland with her own baby. And she takes advantage of a group of teenage girls for free baby-sitting."

Nicki paused with the spoon halfway to Rosalind's mouth, and the baby squealed when it became apparent she would have to wait for another spoonful of peaches. "Could that be true?" Nicki asked aloud, giving Rosalind another mouthful of fruit. "Why, that almost makes me mad!"

"It makes *you* mad?" Laura huffed. "I'm the one the kid threw up on! I'm furious!"

"It's just a theory," Meredith said, shrugging. "But a lot of pieces do fit into the story. It would be awfully convenient for Bridget to do something like this."

"I'm going to go back there and give her a piece of my mind," Laura said, standing. "Let me by, Nicki, I'm going to talk to that flight attendant."

"We don't know anything for sure," Nicki protested, tugging on Laura's sleeve. "Wait a while, please."

"I'm tired of sitting here doing nothing," Laura complained, yanking her arm out of Nicki's grasp. "But okay, I won't accuse her, I'll just go talk to her. I'll ask her about her baby girl, and ask where she is, and who she finds to baby-sit her while she's flying."

"Well, I guess that would be okay," Nicki admitted, scraping another spoonful of peaches from the jar. "Just be careful and watch what you say, okay?"

Laura rolled her eyes and scooted past Kim toward the aisle. "Trust me, Nicki. I'm always tactful."

Fourteen

Laura had not been gone five minutes when she returned, practically falling over Kim into her seat. "Nicki," she whispered, her eyes glittering as she sat in her place. "There's a man on board this plane with a gun. And what's more, he knows I know he's got a gun!"

"What?" Nicki said, turning to Laura. Meredith let her book drop to the floor and leaned in to hear Laura's story.

"Don't anybody turn around!" Laura hissed, keeping her head riveted toward the front of the plane. "I was on my way back to talk to Bridget, when the plane hit an air pocket or something and bumped us. I lost my balance and fell on a guy, and as I put my hand out to catch myself, I felt a gun through his coat!"

"That's impossible," Meredith said, leaning back in exasperation. "You can't get on a plane with a gun in your pocket. You'd set off the metal detectors at the security checkpoints."

"Unless you have a permit to carry a gun," Nicki added, calmly feeding Rosalind. "Maybe he's a sky cop, or a secret agent, or even airline security. Those people are allowed to carry guns."

"I don't think so," Laura hissed, afraid to move. "Remember in the airport when we were trying to figure out people's jobs? This is the guy I said was a loser, and he sure doesn't look like a cop. He's got beady eyes and long hair, and he glared at me when I touched him. Honestly, I think if I hadn't run away, he would have jerked me down in the seat next to him."

Nicki laughed, and Laura tossed her head in anger. "I mean it, Nicki Holland! I'm not kidding! We're all in big trouble!"

"Calm down, Laura, and tell me which guy he is," Meredith said calmly. "Just to set your mind at ease, I'll go ask him what he's up to. We can't have you freaking out and causing a panic."

"I'm not freaking out!" Laura shrieked. Several people in nearby seats turned around to stare at her.

"That does it." Meredith leaned forward and swiveled her head to look at the rows behind them. "Which guy is he?"

"The long-haired guy in the b-br-brown overcoat behind us," Laura stammered. "Sitting by himself on the right side of the plane."

Meredith stood and leaned casually against her seat as she scanned the rear of the plane. "Okay, I see him," she whispered, ducking down to Laura's level. "Now, chill out and don't scream or yell, okay? I'll be back in a minute."

Meredith stepped into the aisle and sauntered toward the rear of the plane. She had to cut through a galley passageway at the back of the plane to get to the right side, but by the time Nicki finished feeding the baby, Meredith had paused by the young man in the brown overcoat.

Nicki handed Rosalind to Kim and raised herself higher by sitting on one leg. Peering behind her, she saw Meredith smile and whisper something to the young man, who listened with a stony face. His arms were folded across his chest, and one thick hand pinched a chewed-up pencil.

"I can't see much," Nicki whispered to Kim and Laura. "But I can tell you that he doesn't look exactly thrilled by what Meredith's saying." Nicki shrugged. "But then again, if he's an undercover cop or something, he's probably not happy that Meredith knows what he is."

Nicki peeked back at the man again. He stared up at Meredith, then he raised his free hand and motioned for Meredith to lean toward him. Nicki saw a flicker of doubt cross Meredith's face, but she bent carefully forward and leaned down as if to hear a secret.

"Are you sure that's smart, Meredith?" Nicki whispered, then her heart skipped a beat as she saw the young man's hand fly toward Meredith's collar.

Before Nicki could shout a warning, the strange young man leaped from his seat with his arm around Meredith's throat. "Nobody move," he shouted to the other startled passengers. He pulled a dark gun from a pocket inside his coat and brandished the weapon above his head. The man paused and closed his eyes. "For the liberty of Northern Ireland, I claim this plane for the Peaceful Resistance Movement!"

Laura screamed and slipped from her seat to the floor. Kim clutched Rosalind tighter, and Nicki ducked behind her tall seat. What had Meredith stumbled into?

As the passengers cowered in their seats, Bridget stepped forward until she stood right in front of the man. "I'm Bridget, and I'd like to help you," she said, a stiff smile on her face. "Why don't you let the girl go and tell us what you want. Would you like the captain to radio someone with a message? I'd be happy to help you in any way I can."

"She sounds like she's offering him coffee and Danish," Laura complained from her hiding place on the floor. "How can she be so nice and calm? That guy's a terrorist!"

"Flight attendants are trained for situations like this," Nicki answered, trying to imitate Bridget's calm even though her heart was thumping so wildly that she could see her necklace pulsing against her shirt.

"Nicki, you take the baby," Kim whispered, passing Rosalind over Laura. "I am closer to him than you are, and I am afraid that gun might go off."

Nicki gathered Rosalind in her arms and shrank lower in her seat. Would that guy actually pull the trigger? Even a tiny hole in a pressurized jet cabin could cause serious trouble. She'd seen too many movies where suitcases and papers and people flew out of ruptured airplanes after a single shot.

"How'd he get the gun?" Kim asked. "No way he could have made it through security with a gun in his jacket."

"Maybe," Nicki whispered back, "someone hid it on the plane and told him where to find it. He's at the very back, you know."

"I'm not going to let the girl go," the young man bellowed.

"But take me to the pilot. I have a message for those who would continue to bring trouble to Northern Ireland."

"Since you are with the Peaceful Resistance Movement, I'm sure you'll want to put that gun away," Bridget said, crossing her arms. "And I'll walk you up front, but the cockpit is locked. The captain will not open it."

"Just take me up there, woman!"

Bridget led the way and the young man followed her, waving the gun in a widening arc as he moved through the plane. As the other passengers screamed and ducked, Meredith shuffled beside him, her head still locked under his strong arm. Her wide eyes met Nicki's, and she mouthed a word that Nicki couldn't recognize.

"Laura, did you see what Meredith said as she went by?" Nicki whispered.

"Are you kidding?" Laura answered. "I'm not lifting my head until all this is over."

"I saw, but I couldn't understand her," Kim said. "It looked like she was trying to say 'plow stand.'"

"Plow stand?" What's a plow stand?"

"Do you think she was trying to say 'ex-plo-sive'?" Kim asked, her brows lifting the question. "Is it possible Meredith knows the guy is wired with explosives?"

Fifteen

For five silent minutes after Meredith, Bridget, and the gun-waving hijacker disappeared through the curtains that separated the coach section from the front of the airplane, Nicki tried to relax in her seat. She was just a kid, and even though she and her friends had solved some pretty grown-up mysteries, she didn't want to be involved in a case of international terrorism. What could she do, especially if Kim was right about explosives? Nicki felt herself begin to shiver like she always did when she saw an intense movie. But this was no movie—they were actually involved in something that would probably land in the headlines of newspapers around the world.

Nicki leaned into the aisle, but she couldn't see what was happening at the front of the plane. Was Meredith okay? Would the pilot unlock his security door?

The silence was broken by the scratchy sound of the pilot's voice over the intercom. "Ladies and gentleman, this is Captain Harris speaking," the pilot's voice echoed through the quiet plane. "One of our passengers, Mr. Owen Dobson, has asked me to turn the plane toward Bermuda. Since Mr. Dobson is holding a hostage, it appears that in the next few hours we will be landing in Bermuda instead of Atlanta. We apologize for the inconvenience."

Laura breathed a sigh of relief and climbed back into her seat. "At least we'll be landing," she said, snapping her seat belt at her waist. "I thought for a minute that crazy guy was going to shoot up the plane."

"What about Meredith?" Kim asked, her eyes wide with concern. "What's he going to do with Meredith?"

Nicki whirled around when she felt a hand descend on her shoulder. Christine stood in front of Meredith's empty seat, her face still faintly flushed. "I saw the whole thing," she said. "I'd have been over sooner, but Fiona fainted when that guy started yelling. One of the flight attendants brought her some smelling salts, and she's okay now. But where did that guy take Meredith?"

"I don't know," Nicki answered, looking toward the front of the plane. "I guess one of us should go up there and see what's going on."

Kim unsnapped her seat belt. "I will go."

"I'll go with you," Nicki said, glancing at Laura. Laura's eyes were tightly closed. "Laura, I need you to take Rosalind. I can't carry her up there with that guy on the loose."

"No, you can't leave her with me," Laura said, throwing her hands up. "Honestly, Nicki, I'm so scared I'm liable to lock myself in the bathroom. I can't be responsible for her, not now."

Nicki looked around in despair. She couldn't leave the baby with Christine—she was too sick.

"I guess I'll take her up with me," Nicki said, standing.

"Maybe Mrs. Cushman will hold the baby. Come on, Kim, let's go see what that guy has done with Meredith."

Although several passengers called for them to sit down and not make trouble, Nicki and Kim walked toward the front of the plane. There was no sign of Meredith, Bridget, or the man in the first-class section, but Nicki could tell they had passed through the area. The passengers in the first-class section were buzzing like those in the coach cabin, even Thad Thumford, the action-adventure film star. He was hiding on the floor, his wig askew on his head.

Only Maureen Sullivan seemed unfazed by the unusual events. She held her tape recorder in her hand and was furiously dictating. "As soon as it is safe to proceed," Nicki heard her say, "I'm moving in to record the gunman's thoughts and motives."

The gunman! Nicki shuddered. It was unnerving to think of her friend in the hands of a gunman.

"Girls! What are you going here?" Mrs. Cushman whispered as Nicki and Kim moved through the first-class section. "And where in the world is that baby's mother?"

"We came up to check on Meredith," Kim answered, sitting for a moment in the empty seat next to Mrs. Cushman. "We could not let her just walk away without trying to do something."

"The best thing to do is ride this thing out." Mrs. Cushman wiped an anxious tear from her eye. "Is Laura okay?"

"Laura's fine," Nicki answered, jiggling the baby in her arms.

Rosalind squirmed as if she were uncomfortable, then she began to fuss.

"Nicki, you've got to do something with that baby," Mrs. Cushman said. "Make her hush! That guy's right behind that door ahead of us, and he's nervous. Don't give him a reason to come out here and get nasty!"

Nicki took an empty seat across from Kim and jiggled the baby on her knees. "Okay, Rosalind, let's go riding," she said, trying to remember all the games she used to play with her little brother and sister. "Want to ride a horsey? Want me to swing you around in my arms?"

Apparently, Rosalind didn't care for games of any kind, because she screwed up her face and began to wail in earnest. "Would you shut that kid up?" Maureen Sullivan yelled over the sound of the baby's crying, and at that instant the door to the cockpit opened and slammed against the wall.

"What's all that racket?" Owen Dobson waved his gun at the first-class passengers. Mrs. Cushman screamed and Maureen Sullivan froze with her tape recorder in her hand. Thad Thumford, the strong man of the movies, lay flat on the floor and covered his head with his hands.

Nicki shushed the baby and raised her head slowly, relieved that Meredith wasn't still pinned in the gunman's grasp.

"I'm sorry about the noise," Nicki called. "The baby's tired and fussy. She doesn't understand everything that's going on and—"

Owen Dobson stomped forward until he stood in front of Nicki. "Nobody would want a baby to get hurt." He stretched out his hand. "Why don't you hand me that baby and I'll send the girl out."

"I—I can't—" Nicki stammered, clutching Rosalind close. Her mind reeled. Would Meredith hate her for not accepting his deal? But how could she hand a helpless baby to a man with a gun?

"I'll make it easy for you," Owen Dobson barked. He brought the gun near the baby's head, and as Nicki froze, he lifted Rosalind from Nicki's arms. Nicki shuddered as he cradled the tiny child. Rosalind stopped crying and stared at the shiny gun. When the baby playfully reached for the black barrel, Nicki felt the cabin swirl around her. Was this how it felt to faint?

Owen Dobson's rough voice jerked Nicki back to consciousness. "You, kid, get out of there," he yelled. He pointed his gun toward Meredith and motioned for her to move out of the tiny cockpit. Meredith stepped slowly into the first-class cabin. Still holding the baby, Owen climbed back into the cockpit and closed the door behind him.

Kim rushed to Meredith's side. "Are you okay?" Meredith nodded slowly and sank into the nearest seat. "Is he really wired with explosives?" Kim whispered, kneeling in the aisle next to Meredith. "Is he going to blow up the plane?"

Meredith knitted her brows. "Explosives? Who said anything about explosives?"

"We thought you did," Nicki said, coming to Meredith's side. "What was it you said as he pulled you toward the cockpit? We couldn't read your lips."

"I said plastic," Meredith answered. "That gun's plastic. That's why the metal detectors didn't pick it up."

Nicki crinkled her nose. "Are you trying to tell me he's hijacking this plane with a toy gun?"

"I don't know," Meredith answered. "It could be a toy or it could be a new kind of gun that I heard about on television. Some terrorists are manufacturing plastic guns for the simple reason that they can evade metal detectors."

"How do we find out if it's a toy or not?" Kim looked around. "I don't want to wait until he tries to shoot somebody."

"I don't want him to hurt the baby," Nicki said. "We've got to get her away from him, and fast!"

Meredith thought a moment, then snapped her fingers. "I have an idea," she said, rising out of her seat. "If we play our cards right, we may find all the answers we're looking for."

Sixteen

3:31 PM Eastern Standard Time

"You want to use my *what*?" Maureen Sullivan lowered her chin and looked doubtfully at Meredith. "Do you even know how to use it?"

"Trust me, I know how to use a laptop," Meredith answered firmly. "I need yours to stop this Owen guy. But it will only help it if has a modem."

"It's top-of-the-line; it has everything." Ms. Sullivan pulled her briefcase into her lap. "And I'll let you use it on one condition: I get exclusive coverage of this story. When we land, you talk to no other reporters."

"Fine." Meredith waved in frustration. "Just let me borrow the computer, please."

Maureen Sullivan opened her briefcase and pulled out a small laptop, which she handed to Meredith. Meredith slipped quietly to the wall behind the cockpit where an in-flight telephone had been installed. "I need one other thing," she whispered to Nicki. "A credit card. Ask Mrs. Cushman if we can use hers for this call."

Maureen Sullivan fished a gold credit card out of her wallet. "You can use mine."

Nicki took the card and Meredith slipped it into the telephone. In a moment, she had the telephone plugged into the

93

computer, and her fingers flew over the keyboard. Nicki slipped around behind Meredith to read the computer screen:

WELCOME TO WORLD KNOWLEDGE COMPUTER
DATABASE
ENTER PASSWORD

Meredith typed a series of characters that did not register on the screen.

PASSWORD ACCEPTED.
ENTER SEARCH PHRASE OR CODE.

Nicki watched in fascination as Meredith typed.

FIND PEACEFUL RESISTANCE MOVEMENT AND
NORTHERN IRELAND OR OWEN DOBSON.

The computer's cursor blinked for a moment, then Nicki read:

0 ENTRIES PEACEFUL RESISTANCE MOVEMENT
144297 ENTRIES NORTHERN IRELAND
0 ENTRIES PEACEFUL RESISTANCE MOVEMENT
AND NORTHERN IRELAND
1 ENTRY OWEN DOBSON

"Interesting." Meredith studied the screen. "I had a hunch this might be the case."

"A hunch about what?" Nicki whispered.

"There is no Peaceful Resistance Movement," Meredith answered. "Owen Dobson made it up. No matter what he says, he's not affiliated with anyone, unless the organization formed overnight and no one knows about it."

"Are you sure?" Nicki asked. "What is this thing you're talking to, anyway?"

"The most up-to-date database in the world," Meredith answered. "Believe me, if there is a Peaceful Resistance Movement, this database would have record of it."

Meredith typed once again, and Nicki leaned closer for a better look at the keyboard.

PRINT ENTRY OWEN DOBSON.

The cursor blinked again for a moment, then a paragraph of information filled the computer screen so rapidly Nicki couldn't read it. Meredith waited until the computer had stopped scrolling, then she typed SAVE ENTRY, DISCONNECT. After a moment, Meredith hung up the phone, retrieved the gold credit card, and carried the computer back to Maureen Sullivan.

"Now we see who Owen Dobson is," Meredith said, typing again. Maureen Sullivan watched in amazement as Meredith retrieved the information she had saved in the computer. Slowly, in a more readable form, the story filled the computer screen.

LOCAL YOUTH MOURNS FATHER KILLED IN RANDOM VIOLENCE

The Belfast Register
March 23, 1993

Reginald Sean Dobson, 60, died yesterday in random violence allegedly sponsored by the Irish Republican Army. A car bomb outside a Belfast library exploded, killing Reginald Dobson as he and his son walked along the city sidewalk. Owen Dobson, 27, was hospitalized with minor injuries.

"That has to be it," Meredith said after reading the news article. "Even though it happened a long time ago, Owen Dobson was disturbed by his father's murder. This action today may be his way of trying to draw attention to his father's death."

Maureen Sullivan lifted an elegant brow. "So he's not a terrorist?"

Meredith shook her head. "I think he meant to inspire terror, but there is no Peaceful Resistance Movement. If there was, I don't think they'd be going around hijacking airplanes or taking babies hostage."

"They'd be peaceful," Kim said. "This guy is anything but."

"That's quite a theory." Maureen Sullivan snapped her tape

recorder off. "But how do you intend to test it? Short of going into that cockpit and calling his bluff, there's nothing you can do. Remember, he's holding a gun on a baby."

"And if the gun went off, the entire plane could go down," Nicki added. "What if he accidentally shot the pilots? I don't think Bridget knows how to fly the airplane."

"We'll just have to go to Bermuda and see what this guy wants," Maureen Sullivan said, taking the computer from Meredith. "If it's publicity he wants, he can tell his story to me and I'll relay it to the press." She smiled. "This could be my big break onto national television."

Something in Maureen Sullivan's attitude made Nicki feel sick. She closed her eyes and imagined what her parents would think when her flight didn't arrive in Tampa. What would they do when they turned on CNN and saw Nicki's plane stranded at an airport in Bermuda? What would her little brother and sister say when they heard that Nicki and the other passengers were under the control of a deranged man and might not even be coming home?

"There has to be a way out of this, dear God," she prayed quietly under her breath. "A way without anyone getting hurt. Please, God, do whatever you have to do to get us home safely."

Seventeen

"There is at least one good thing," Kim said after a long silence. For the last twenty minutes there had been no sound from the cockpit—no announcements from the captain, no reassurances from Bridget, and no sounds of a baby crying.

"What's good about this?" Meredith asked, staring straight ahead at the wall separating first class from Owen Dobson.

"If Bridget is Rosalind's mother, she is in there with her baby. If she is the baby's guardian, then she is in the best place to guard the baby."

Nicki and Meredith looked at one another. In the last hour, neither had thought much about their search for Rosalind's mother.

"Kim's right," Meredith said, snapping her fingers. "How weird it all is! But if Bridget is Rosalind's mother—"

"What if she's not the baby's mother?" Nicki said. "This may be the best time to flush out the guardian or whoever left us that box for Rosalind. Remember what you said earlier? You said if the baby was in danger—"

"I don't think she could ever be in more danger than this," Meredith said, standing. "But no one else on board knows that Owen Dobson has the baby."

Nicki moved out into the aisle. "So let's tell them."

Kim thrust her leg into the aisle to block Meredith and Nicki. "There's only one problem."

"What?" Meredith asked.

"You said it would be dangerous for anyone to confront the man with the gun," Kim pointed out. "If you stir the baby's guardian to action, won't you be sending him or her into a dangerous situation? Shouldn't we leave things as they are for now?"

Nicki felt her heart sink. Kim was right, of course. If they ran through the plane screaming that the gunman had taken the baby hostage, surely whoever was watching over the baby would freak out and try to do something, maybe even something dangerous or foolish.

"And there's always the possibility that Bridget is the baby's guardian," Meredith said, nodding at Nicki. "All we'd do by spreading the word is cause panic. Everything's calm now—maybe we should leave things alone."

Nicki reluctantly agreed and sank back into a seat.

Eighteen

A pretty flight attendant walked through first class and hesi-
tantly knocked on the door of the cockpit. Owen Dobson
opened the door, scowling, and Nicki sighed in relief when
she saw Rosalind sleeping in his arms.

"We'd like to know if we can serve the afternoon snack," the
flight attendant asked. "The passengers are hungry, and we'll
be in the air for at least two more hours before we land in
Bermuda."

"Sure, serve it, but serve us first," Owen Dobson growled,
grasping the door handle. "And no funny business! You bring the
food here and hand it through to Bridget—she'll give it to me."

"Whatever you say," the flight attendant said, moving away
to the galley. A few moments later she and another attendant
appeared and handed trays with steaming bowls of tomato
soup and crackers with cheese through the cockpit door.

"Do you think they thought of blinding that guy's eyes with
the hot soup?" Meredith whispered to Nicki. "All Bridget would
have to do is act like she slipped and spill the hot soup on him."

"If she spilled it on him, the hot soup would burn the baby,
too," Nicki reminded Meredith. "I don't think he's going to put
Rosalind down."

"I forgot about the baby," Meredith admitted. "Taking her

was a fiendish move on his part, because now everyone will listen to him. Nobody wants to hurt a baby."

"Except Fiona," Nicki said, recalling Fiona's bitter attitude. She suddenly grasped Meredith's arm. "Do you suppose Fiona said all those ugly things about babies because she's the baby's mother? I know she's young, but she's old enough to have had a baby."

"Maybe she was using reverse psychology to convince herself that she hates babies when she really loves them," Meredith said. "I suppose your theory is a possibility."

"Or maybe she was being negative just to throw us off her trail," Kim added. "But from where she was sitting behind us, she could easily keep an eye on Rosalind."

"Christine told me that Fiona actually fainted when the gunman stood up," Nicki said. "If you were watching over a baby and a demented guy with a gun stood up only a couple of rows behind her, wouldn't you be upset? Upset enough to faint?"

"Maybe," Meredith said. She looked at Nicki curiously. "So what are you going to do?"

"I'm going to go back there and tell Fiona the baby's all right," Nicki said, unbuckling her seat belt. "I'm not going to scare her or anything, but I want her to know Rosalind's fine. We don't hear anything from the baby because she's asleep."

"You'd better hurry," Kim said, looking down the aisle. "Here comes the food cart, and you won't get through if you don't go now."

Nicki managed to squeeze past the food cart as it pulled out of the galley, and she walked quickly back to the cabin where Christine and Laura sat in their seats under a cloud of gloom. Laura's face was as pale as paper, and, in a remarkable contrast, Christine's face shone pink with fever.

"You two are a sight," Nicki remarked, pausing at their seats. "How are you doing?"

"Okay," Christine mumbled, not opening her eyes.

"Is it almost over?" Laura whispered, gripping the arms of her seat. "Is my mom okay?"

"Everyone's fine," Nicki said calmly, loud enough for the other passengers to hear. "We're just flying to Bermuda, and I guess everything's going to be okay."

"Where's the man with the gun?" an older man demanded from several rows in front of Laura. "What's the pilot doing?"

"Owen Dobson is the man with the gun," Nicki answered, carefully turning toward the man who asked the question, "and he's in the cockpit with the flight attendant and the pilots. It's been quiet up there."

"Where's the baby you were carrying?"

A woman asked the question, and Nicki whirled around to see who had spoken. But a sea of curious and expectant faces waited to hear her answer, and there was no way to tell who had asked the question.

"Um, the man has the baby," she answered. Then she added, "But the baby's okay. She's sleeping."

A murmur of concern rippled throughout the crowd, and Nicki tried to smile. "Everything's going to be okay, I think." She nodded with more confidence than she felt. "We just have to wait until we land in Bermuda."

She moved quickly to the seat where Fiona sat looking out the window. Fiona turned to Nicki without surprise, as if she had been expecting her.

"You're lying, aren't you?" Fiona asked simply. "You don't know that everything's going to be okay. You're just saying those things to keep everybody calm. That's what the flight attendants have been saying, too, and they don't know anything."

"I have to believe things will be okay," Nicki answered. "I believe that God's going to take care of us."

Fiona snorted. "Well, God has put me in some pretty ugly messes before," she said, rolling her eyes. "I haven't seen Him reaching out to help me lately."

Nicki tilted her head. "God doesn't put us into trouble," she explained, "but sometimes He allows us to feel the pain of trouble we get ourselves into." Nicki laughed. "At least, that's what my parents tell me when they ground me for something stupid I did."

Fiona folded her arms and turned toward the window again.

"Anyway, I just wanted you to know that the baby's okay," Nicki said, pausing. "The guy took the baby because he figured no one would want to see Rosalind get hurt. With what we've found out about Owen Dobson, I can't believe he'd really hurt her."

"I told you, I don't care about that baby," Fiona snapped, turning her shoulder to Nicki. "Now please leave me alone."

"I know you say you don't care about her," Nicki whispered in a voice that only Fiona could hear. "But I know you do. Don't give her up, Fiona, not this way. Don't abandon the precious life God has given you."

Nicki stood up and moved away, pausing only for a moment when she heard Fiona break into loud, heartbreaking sobs.

Nineteen

"That settles it for me," Nicki announced as she joined Meredith and Kim in the first-class section. "I told Fiona not to abandon her baby, and she burst into tears. I would have gone back, but she needs some time to think things through, I think."

"She really said Rosalind was her baby?" Meredith asked, her eyes wide. "I thought for sure Bridget would prove to be our missing mother."

"No, it's Fiona," Nicki said. "Though she still won't admit it. She keeps denying everything, but why would she be so upset if Rosalind wasn't her kid? She's just going through some struggles or something. She probably feels she's too young to raise a baby."

"She could make an adoption plan for Rosalind," Kim suggested. "I know a friend who was adopted from Korea, and she is very grateful to have the chance to grow up with two strong parents."

"That would be better than dumping Rosalind off in America," Nicki said. "For sure."

The plane hit an air pocket and Nicki gripped the arms of her seat. "Things are getting rough," she said, feeling her stomach flip-flop. "I hope we're not flying through a storm."

"As long as Owen Dobson isn't wrestling the pilot for the steering wheel, we should be okay," Meredith said, searching for the end of her seat belt. "But we should fasten ourselves in, anyway."

"Ladies and gentlemen, we are flying through some rough weather en route to Bermuda," the pilot's voice rang over the intercom. "Please bear with us as we attempt to fly up and out of the turbulence. Please remain in your seats and do not move about the cabin."

The flight attendants rushed to secure the food carts in the galleys, then they strapped themselves into their seats. The flight grew steadily rougher, and several times Nicki could actually feel the vibrations of the plane's wings as it jostled among the clouds like a giant bird with arthritis.

"If that guy doesn't kill us with his gun, he'll wreck us in this storm," Maureen Sullivan wailed after one particularly rough bump. "We weren't prepared for this kind of weather. We probably don't have enough fuel to ride this storm out."

"Don't say that!" Mrs. Cushman yelled, covering her ears. "You're scaring me!"

In the midst of their fear and the rough weather, a single small figure moved up the aisle toward the cockpit door. It was a woman, coming slowly and steadily despite the rough ride. As the woman moved forward, clinging to the seat backs for support, Nicki finally recognized her as Megan O'Connor, the woman Mrs. Cushman had met in the airport lobby.

Meredith followed Nicki's gaze. "What's she doing here?"

Nicki shook her head.

Megan O'Connor made her way to the cockpit door, straightened her shoulders, and knocked firmly.

"Who's there?" Owen Dobson demanded, opening the door a few inches. Through the narrow opening, Nicki saw the gleam of his gun.

"I simply cannot go to Bermuda," Megan O'Connor said. "I must meet my husband in Atlanta. I haven't seen him for over a year, and he's waiting there for me. He'll be frantic if this plane doesn't come in on time, and you simply must allow us to continue on our intended journey."

Megan O'Connor's brave speech and sheer audacity surprised Owen Dobson. His jaw dropped and he opened the door wider, revealing Bridget, the wary pilots, and Rosalind, still sleeping in the crook of the gunman's arm.

"Lady, are you nuts?" Dobson demanded, waving his gun. "Sit down and shut up, or I'll blow you off this plane."

"No, you won't." Megan O'Connor stretched herself to her full height and resolutely reached for the gun with both hands. Dobson opened his mouth to protest, but he was caught off guard by Megan's attack and hampered by the baby in his free arm. As they struggled for possession of the weapon, Nicki heard a quiet click.

Someone pulled the trigger. And nothing happened.

The worthless gun hit the carpeted floor with a dull thud. Megan O'Connor glared at Dobson. "You tried to hijack this plane with a toy?" she asked, lifting her chin.

"I've still got this baby," Dobson answered, holding Rosalind above the floor. "Stand back or I'll drop her."

But Dobson stood sandwiched between the cockpit doorway and Megan O'Connor. When he thrust the baby forward to threaten Rosalind, he practically placed the baby in Megan O'Connor's arms.

Dobson wheeled and retreated into the cockpit, where he nearly ran into Bridget. "Give me the baby," she said, holding out her hands. "You don't want to hurt that girl, so give her to me."

Rosalind, her blue eyes wide and startled, began to cry.

Meredith jumped to take advantage of the moment. "You didn't want your father to be hurt, did you, Mr. Dobson?" she called, standing. "We know how he died. We know how you must feel." The plane lurched as it hit a pocket of air turbulence. Dobson staggered and stared at Meredith as if she had suddenly sprouted wings.

Maureen Sullivan smelled the climax of her story and sprang to her feet. "We know about your father, Reginald Sean Dobson," she called, moving into Dobson's line of vision. "We know he died in Belfast. We know you feel helpless and you want to do something. But this is not the right thing to do, Owen. Hurting these other people won't bring your father back."

—

Dobson, fearless terrorist and confused young man, silently placed baby Rosalind in Bridget's arms. Then he buried his face in his hands and began to cry.

The pilot spoke over his shoulder. "Get him out of here," he said, "and we'll make a beeline for Atlanta. We'll have a doctor waiting at the gate."

"A doctor?" Kim whispered to Nicki. "But no one was hurt."

"A psychologist," Nicki answered as Maureen Sullivan led Dobson to a row of empty seats. "That guy needs help."

She turned to congratulate Megan O'Connor for her bravery in disarming the hijacker, but the little Irish woman had already left the cabin.

Twenty

". . . and in 1500 B.C. in Egypt, a shaved head was considered the ultimate in feminine beauty," Meredith told Nicki, Laura, Christine, Kim, and Rosalind. "Egyptian women removed every hair from their heads with gold tweezers and polished their chrome domes with buffing cloths."

Kim giggled. "Can you imagine buffing your head?"

"It doesn't sound any stranger than anything else we've seen today." Nicki glanced again at the forward seat where Dobson sat handcuffed to the tall police officer who had come forward after things had quieted down. The policeman showed the pilots his badge and took custody of Owen Dobson for the remainder of the flight.

Rosalind played happily on Kim's lap. "I can't believe we'll still be stepping off this plane with Rosalind," Nicki said, feeling a little sad. "I can't believe that Fiona is still denying she's Rosalind's mother."

"I can't believe Bridget laughed until her side hurt when we asked if Rosalind was her baby," Laura added. "But at least she said she'd help us find the right people to take care of Rosalind when we land. But I'll still worry about her."

Meredith snapped her fingers. "I think I've figured it out,"

110

she said, looking at Nicki. "We know there's a guardian for the baby on this plane, right?"

"Sure," Nicki answered. "Because of the box of supplies someone left for us."

"We're forgetting the other story," Meredith went on. "Moses' sister was his guardian, but remember the story of Solomon?"

"What is she talking about?" Christine asked, brushing her damp bangs from her hot forehead. "Am I missing something?"

"I don't know," Nicki answered. "What about Solomon? Two mothers were fighting over one baby. The false mother was willing to let the child be cut in half, but the real mother—"

"The real mother dared to interrupt the king and protest his royal decree and decision," Meredith pointed out. "She threw herself at the king's feet and said she'd be glad to give the baby up if the king would spare the child's life."

"So?" Laura quipped. "No one was threatening to cut Rosalind in half. And there weren't two mothers arguing over her."

"No," Nicki said, grinning when she realized what Meredith was thinking, "but one woman dared to interrupt our hijacker and protest his decision. She had the guts to actually fight for his gun and she risked her life to save the baby's."

"That short Irish woman?" Laura frowned. "Megan what's-her-name?"

"Megan O'Connor," Nicki whispered. "And I know where she's sitting. She's been right behind Fiona the entire flight."

Nicki gathered Rosalind into her arms and slipped the diaper bag over her wrist. With Meredith, Kim, and Laura following her, she walked down the aisle until she was standing next to Megan O'Connor. Mrs. O'Connor put down her newspaper and smiled at the girls.

"We wanted to thank you for your bravery up there a while ago," Nicki said, noticing how the woman's gaze flitted over Rosalind. "We owe you a lot."

"Bah, 'twas nothing," Megan answered, lifting her paper.

"There's something else," Meredith said, nodding toward Rosalind. "Your daughter needs you. Don't make us hand her over to the authorities when we reach Atlanta. She'd much rather be with you."

Megan O'Connor gasped, then her eyes filled with tears and her chin quivered. "How—who—"

Nicki smiled as Rosalind reached out her arms to the woman she knew as mother.

Nicki placed the baby in Mrs. O'Connors arms. "We knew only a mother who really loves her baby would do what you did up there in the cockpit," Nicki explained. "And though we don't know why you felt you had to leave Rosalind, we know you can find help somehow if you need it. Just don't abandon her this way."

Megan O'Connor shook her head. "I've been apart from my husband for over a year," she said, wiping tears from her cheeks. "He's in Atlanta, and I had to wait months to get a permanent visa to the United States. I couldn't bring myself to tell him we've got another mouth to feed, because he's always telling me how tough things are in his new job. I thought if I gave Rosalind the same chance to start a new life in America that we have—"

"You can find people to help you," Laura suggested. "I've got relatives in Atlanta, and their church is always helping people. They could sponsor you and help y'all out until you get settled and on your feet."

"Do you really think it's possible?" Megan O'Connor asked, hugging Rosalind close. "I didn't know how we would cope in the United States. I hear things about poverty and trouble and I didn't think we could afford to have a child—"

"The United States is a land of opportunity for those who work hard," Kim said, nodding at Mrs. O'Connor. "My family came from Korea two years ago. We do not regret coming here."

Mrs. O'Connor hugged her daughter tightly as tears ran down her cheeks. "Oh, darling, I'm so sorry," she whispered, rocking back and forth with the baby. "I can't believe I nearly walked away from you."

"Who was the woman in the airport?" Meredith asked. "The woman who actually gave us the baby?"

"My sister," Mrs. O'Connor said, opening her eyes. "She came up with the idea to bring the baby over on the plane with someone who wouldn't suspect anything. Of course, I wouldn't give Rosalind up unless I could be sure she was okay, so my sister Mary gave you the baby in the airport. She told me I was crazy for taking a baby to America. She never wanted me to marry Michael, and then when I got pregnant, she warned me not to tell him about the baby."

"I think you'll find she was wrong," Laura said. "I'm sure your husband will love baby Rosalind as much as you do. Just give him a chance to get to know her." Laura reached out and patted Rosalind's chubby cheek. "We've only known her a few hours, and we all love her a lot."

"A lot," echoed Nicki. "She's a real treasure, Mrs. O'Connor. We're going to miss her."

Megan O'Connor hugged her baby and smelled her clothes. "Oh, how I missed her," she said, sighing. "I don't think I could have gone through with it. I've been struggling the entire flight, wondering if I'd have the nerve to get off this plane and not look back. I don't think I could have done it."

"I'm glad we found you," Laura said, patting the baby. "But I don't know how *we're* going to get off this plane and not look back. I don't know if I can do it."

"You can," Nicki said, grabbing Laura's elbow. She nodded a farewell to Mrs. O'Connor and pushed Laura gently down the aisle back to their seats. "You're too young to take care of a baby full time."

"You can't even handle a little case of baby vomit," Meredith pointed out. "What would you do if the baby had a serious case of dirty diaper or something?"

"Why, I'd call one of you, of course," Laura replied with a

graceful toss of her head. She slipped through the row to her seat. "After all, what are best friends for?"

Twenty-one

"Nicki, I think someone had better go check on Fiona," Christine said, tugging on Nicki's sleeve. "She's all huddled up in that seat back there, and she's either sick or still crying."

"She's crying?" Nicki asked, looking around.

"Good grief, we're landing in less than twenty minutes, so can't it wait?" Laura snapped. "Landings always make me nervous. Stay in your seat belt, Nicki."

"I ought to go check on her," Nicki said, unbuckling her seat belt. "After all, she started crying when I thought she was Rosalind's mother. If she's still crying, it can't be about Rosalind."

"I wonder what could be wrong with her?" Meredith looked back at the seat where Fiona sat, her long brown hair hiding her face. "Maybe she was really scared during the hijacking."

Nicki slipped past Meredith into the aisle and padded back to the empty seat next to Fiona. The girl seemed to ignore Nicki for a moment, then she flung her hair back and gazed at Nicki with tear-filled eyes. "What do you want now?" she demanded. "Do you just want to bother me again?"

"I never meant to bother you at all," Nicki said, pulling away. "I just wondered if you wanted to talk about whatever's bothering you. But since you obviously don't—"

"Wait, don't go," Fiona said, reaching out as Nicki pulled away. "I'm sorry, I guess I misjudged you. I thought you knew why I was going to Atlanta, and it made me mad that you had figured it out. I didn't think I was showing."

"Showing what?" Nicki slipped into the empty seat and watched Fiona carefully.

Fiona's hand involuntarily covered her stomach. "I thought you had figured out that I was going to the United States for an abortion. They're illegal in Ireland, you know, and my boyfriend doesn't want to have anything to do with a baby. When you said, 'Don't abandon the precious life God has given you,' well, I just freaked."

Nicki's jaw dropped. "I didn't know you were pregnant," she whispered. "We really thought you were Rosalind's mother."

"When you were talking about unborn babies, you didn't know I was pregnant? You weren't just preaching to make me change my mind?"

"Honest, we had no idea," Nicki answered. "Christine, Meredith, Laura, and I have very strong feelings about abortion." Nicki softened her voice. "We care about girls and their babies. My mom volunteers one morning every week at the crisis pregnancy center in our town. That's where they help girls get medical care, maternity clothes, whatever they need so they don't have to have an abortion. They can keep their babies or make an adoption plan for them. But the babies' lives are saved."

"Really?" Fiona sounded doubtful. "You know, I was angry at

first when I got pregnant, and really scared. My boyfriend walked out on me, and my parents would absolutely die if I told them, so I put in for a visa to the United States. I was lucky enough to actually get one. I didn't think anyone cared about me, much less about this baby."

"We care," Nicki said. "And if you're not ready to raise a child, there are thousands of couples who are waiting for children to love. You could bring a lifetime of joy to one of them and find a good home for your baby."

"You've really made me think," Fiona said, digging in her purse for a tissue. She paused to blow her nose. "I don't know what I'm going to do, but I'm not calling an abortion clinic right away. I think I'll go to my sister's house and think a while first."

"Call a crisis pregnancy center and get the facts before you do anything," Nicki said. "Promise me you'll do that. And promise me that you'll remember that you're carrying a real baby, not a gob of tissue."

Nicki glanced down at the baggy shirt Fiona wore. "The heart of another person is beating under your skin. Please, let it beat for a long, long time."

Fiona stared at Nicki, then she nodded. "I'll think about what you've said," she said, wiping her nose again. "I promise I will."

The sound of the plane's intercom interrupted their conversation. "Ladies and gentlemen, we are now approaching the Atlanta International Airport. The captain has turned on the

"Fasten Seat Belt" sign, so please return to your seats and secure all seat-back tray tables."

"I'd better go back to my seat," Nicki said.

"Yeah, go on." Fiona waved her tissue as her eyes filled with tears again. "And thanks for everything. I never dreamed this flight would be so . . . eventful."

"Me, either," Nicki said. "And don't forget to think about what I said, okay?"

"I won't," Fiona promised.

—

"In eighteenth-century England, women's wigs were sometimes four feet tall," Meredith said, again consulting the pages of *222 Fabulous Factoids*. "These wigs were dusted with flour and decorated with stuffed birds, plates of fruit, and model ships. They were matted with lard to keep them from coming apart, and mice and insects were always trying to eat them."

"That's absolutely, totally, and inconceivably disgusting," Laura said, crinkling her nose. "Meredith, how much would I have to pay you to toss that book out the window?"

"More money than you'll ever have," Meredith answered. "It's too mesmerizing. Did you know that in medieval Japan, dentists extracted teeth by pulling them out with their fingers? And in 1977, more abortions than tonsillectomies were performed in the United States."

"I hope that fascinating factoid isn't true this year," Nicki said, glancing back at Rosalind. The baby played happily on her mother's lap. "I'm not wild about tonsils, but I sure do love babies."

"Me, too," Laura said, following Nicki's gaze. "Especially when they come with clean clothes, extra diapers, and nannies." She laughed. "Now, if someone could only find a way to keep them from spitting up all over the place—"

"Don't worry about it, Laura," Kim said, her eyes dark and serious. "When you love a baby, you don't mind the smelly stuff."

"It's good our mothers didn't mind, or we wouldn't be here," Nicki said, smiling at her friends. "But I never realized how hard it is to have and take care of a baby. I think the first thing I'll tell my mom when I see her is thanks."

"That's nice," Laura answered. "But that's not what I'm going to say to my mom."

Laura paused, and Nicki, Kim, Christine, and Meredith waited.

"So what are you going to say?" Kim finally asked.

Laura grinned. "I'm going to say, 'Wow, Mom, our trip to Europe was so cool—when can we go back again?"

The Case of the Mystery Mark

Strange things are happening at Pine Grove Middle School. Ever since the new girl came to town, Nicki Holland and her friends have witnessed vandalism, dognapping, stolen papers, and threatening notes. Is there a connection? Nicki and her friends want to find out before something terrible happens to one of them!

About the Author

Angela Hunt lives in Florida with her husband Gary, their two children, and two big dogs that weigh more than she does! Her favorite hobby is reading and she loves to write stories. You can read more about her and her books at www.angelahuntbooks.com.

Angie also reports that Meredith's fabulous factoids are true and come from the book *2201 Fascinating Facts* by David Louis (Greenwich House Publishers, New York, 1983), in case you'd like to read some fabulous fascinating factoids on your own.